Just then th
arrived," the

Nick slid across the . . . . against hers. "There's really only one thing you need to know."

Jessie swallowed, her mouth suddenly dry. "What's that?"

"You're going to be the most beautiful woman in the room."

That was so far away from what she'd expected to hear she wasn't sure she'd heard correctly.

The heat in his sapphire gaze pinned her to the spot. He bent his head down toward hers and her pulse jumped in response. He hovered centimeters away, his eyes still locked on hers.

"I want you more than I've wanted anything in a very long time," he said. "But if you get in my way I'll still crush you like a bug."

Dear Reader

I've had a girl crush on Jessie since I first met her while writing ALL'S FAIR IN LUST & WAR. She burst into my brain fully formed and already begging for her own story.

But that didn't make this book easy to write. Jessie, you see, is very particular. She knows exactly what she will and won't do. And when I wrote something she didn't like she would stomp off to some remote corner of my brain, refusing to come out until I promised to fix it.

The resulting story is one I know you'll love. Jessie is now the owner of her own boutique ad agency in New York City, and when we join her she's on top of the world. She's determined to rule the ad biz—and love is *not* in her plans.

But, as we all know, even the best-laid plans get blown to smithereens when the right man walks in. Nick is the perfect match for Jessie—smart, powerful, and devastatingly handsome (not to mention a fabulous kisser). In fact he has just one flaw—he wants to own her business.

Documenting the fireworks between them was great fun—but hopefully not nearly as much as reading about them will be!

I hope you love Jessie and Nick as much as I do by the time you're done. And I hope you'll join me online to chat about them! My internet home is www.amberpagebooks.com, but you can also find me on Facebook at facebook.com/amberpagebooks, and on Twitter at @amberpagewrites.

Thank you so much for joining me on this journey!

Amber

DATING
THE ENEMY

BY
AMBER PAGE

Published in Great Britain 2015
by Mills & Boon, an imprint of Harlequin (UK) Limited,
Eton House, 18-24 Paradise Road, Richmond, Surrey, TW9 1SR

© 2015 Amber Page

ISBN: 978-0-263-24948-4

Amber Page has been writing stories since—well, since she could write, and still counts the pinning of her *Bubble People* tale to the classroom bulletin board in the third grade as one of her happiest childhood memories.

She's also an avid reader, and has been addicted to romances since she first discovered them on the dusty shelves of her favourite library as a young teen. The nerdy little bookworm she was is still pinching herself to make sure that this whole 'getting published' thing is real.

When not penning happily-ever-afters, Amber works as an advertising writer in the heart of Indiana, where she lives with the love of her life, their daughter, and a menagerie of furry animals. She also blogs, gardens, and sometimes even manages to sneak in a few hours of sleep.

Don't ask her how she does it all. She's too tired to remember.

To my mom and dad, who taught me to believe in
my dreams—and who never stopped chasing their own.

And to my daughter, who'd better not read this for at least
another ten years. Hopefully someday you'll understand
that this is why Mommy's always so tired
(and that it's totally worth it).

PROLOGUE

JESSIE HOVERED ON the edge of the dance floor, feeling strangely melancholy as she watched Becky swirl around the room in her new husband's arms. Gone was the brittle-shelled worker bee of a year ago. In her place was a true beauty, sparkling with happiness.

It seemed her friend had found her white knight—even if he *had* needed a good scrubbing before his true colors showed.

Seeing her joy, Jessie found herself wishing for...*something*. Not a happily-ever-after, but something more substantial than the one-night affairs she usually satisfied herself with.

Unfortunately it was just her and her champagne glass this evening. Might as well drink up.

She lifted the cold glass to her lips and took a big gulp, letting the bubbles dance their way down her throat. It was good champagne. Slightly sweet, smooth as silk. A satisfied purr pushed its way out into the air before she could stop it.

A quiet, thoroughly masculine laugh sounded from beside her.

"Good champagne?" its owner asked.

Jessie looked up...and up...and up.

Towering above her was an escapee from a fashion magazine. Blond-haired, blue-eyed, with shoulders that seemed to stretch from one end of the room to the other. She smiled. Perhaps her night wouldn't be quite so lonely after all.

"Well, it *is* turning out to be a more satisfying wedding

date than I expected," she said. "Good looks. Good taste. No bad dance moves."

He laughed again, and the sound reverberated in her bones.

"And to think, I was just about to ask you to dance," he said. "But something tells me I won't measure up to your bubbly friend, there."

For the first time Jessie let herself hear the music. It was slow and sexy, sung by a man who obviously knew how to get a lady out of her clothes.

She quickly downed the last of her champagne and smiled up at her companion. "Well, would you look at that? It seems he's disappeared. Perhaps you could show me your moves before he comes back? I'm sure he wouldn't mind."

"I'd be happy to," the stranger said, and offered her his arm.

She took it and he swept her out on to the dance floor, smoothly turning her until they faced each other, with one hand nestled in the small of her back.

Jessie's breath hitched as they started to move. This man could *dance*. He took control, gracefully leading her where he wanted to go, his body hovering just centimeters from hers. Jessie gave herself up to his rhythm, barely managing to keep herself from melting into a puddle of goo in his arms.

"My name's Nick, by the way," he said, looking down at her through his lashes.

Jessie was so lost in the hypnotic sway of his body that it took a moment to sink in. When it did, she laughed softly. "I'm Jessie," she said. "And I hope you'll excuse my incoherence. I'm afraid I'm not used to dancing with partners of your caliber."

He grinned. "My father will be glad that the many months of dance lessons he forced me to take have paid off."

"Your dad made you take dance lessons?"

"Yeah. Well, just those of the ballroom kind. We're forced to attend an exhausting number of balls and galas and that kind of thing. It's either dance or die of boredom."

Jessie blinked. "I don't think I've *ever* been invited to a ball. Are you part of one of those super-rich hotel families or something?"

He grimaced. "Nothing that glamorous. Just your average wealthy New York business clan."

Jessie rolled her eyes. "Oh. Right. Because *those* are a dime a dozen."

He shrugged his shoulders. "I'm just glad I can give your champagne a run for its money."

"Yep. You win."

"Oh, you haven't seen anything yet," he said as he sent her out into a dress-twirling spin. He brought her back in a low dip and, when his face was just inches above hers, whispered, "I have all sorts of mind-boggling moves."

Jessie was still trying to decide how to answer that when the first chords of the "Chicken Dance" began to play. The horrified look of confusion on his face made her laugh out loud.

"What? You don't dance the 'Chicken Dance' at your fancy-pants balls?"

"No. Never."

"Well, let me up and I'll show you how it's done."

Nick couldn't help but laugh as the sexy redhead who'd seemed so classy a moment ago began flapping her arms and shimmying downward. When she clucked like a chicken, he gave in to a belly laugh that shook his whole body.

"Come on," she said. "This is no time to be shy. Let your inner chicken loose!"

He considered refusing, but when he looked around the

dance floor and realized that everyone was getting into the action he thought better of it.

Seconds later he was shaking his butt and flapping his arms. This was *fun*. Perhaps he should recommend they include it at the next charity gala. It would certainly be amusing to see his father attempting to bawk like a chicken.

Jessie deliberately bumped his butt with her own deliciously round derrière as she swooped down into another shimmy. He bumped her back, and before long their chicken dance had devolved into a butt-bumping contest.

He drove her further and further off the dance floor with every turn, until finally they bumped into a table. She collapsed into a convenient chair, laughing hysterically.

He sat down beside her, giving in to his own fit of laughter. Every time he thought he might be able to stop he looked at her and collapsed into another laughing spree.

Finally, they were both able to catch their breath. Jessie looked at him with sparkling eyes, her pale cheeks pink with laughter. Seeing the way the fiery tendrils that had escaped from her elegant chignon brought her face to life, he couldn't resist the urge to send more tumbling down.

He quickly picked the bobby pins out of her hair, disintegrating the up-do.

"Hey," she said, frowning up at him. "I didn't say you could do that."

"I know," he said, trying to put an apology in his smile, "but I wanted to see the real you. I'll bet you don't wear your hair up very often."

"Oh, you'd be surprised," she said as she ran her hands through her hair, trying to bring order to the wild mane. "I can be the quintessential businesswoman when I need to be."

"And why would you need to do that? I had you pegged as a creative type."

"I am. But I happen to own my own digital advertising agency. A certain amount of seriousness is required at times."

He sat back, trying not to let her see how much she impressed him. She was certifiably hot. Incredibly funny. And an entrepreneur to boot. *Man*. She might just be his perfect woman.

"Hmm. I might be in need of a digital agency soon. Can I have your card?"

"I'm not in the mood to talk business tonight, but I would like to see more of you." She raked her eyes up and down his body in an unmistakably sensuous manner. "How about I give you my room key instead?"

Every single cell in his body cried *Hell, yes*, but before he could answer the bride swooped down on them.

"Jessie!" she called. "Your services as maid of honor are needed!"

Jessie's face collapsed in disappointment for a split second, but quickly rearranged itself into a smile.

"What? I held your bouquet. Wiped the ring-bearer's spit-up from your gown. Gave a splendid toast. My job here is done!"

Becky pulled on her arm, forcing her up from the chair.

"Nuh-uh. I am about to throw my bouquet. And you, my friend, are going to be in the front row."

"What? No way. I'm busy here."

"*Yes*, way. I'm sure Nick won't mind. You wouldn't want her to shirk her duties…or miss her chance to catch the bouquet, would you?" she asked, giving him a pointed look.

"I don't much care about the bouquet, but I'll let you steal her if you promise to give me her number later," he said.

"You got it. And I won't even make you promise to marry her."

"Good. I'm not the marrying kind."

"Neither am I," said Jessie.

Becky looked at them, a knowing expression on her face. "That's what they all say."

"Cut it out," Jessie answered, swatting her playfully. "Just because you're a blushing bride, it doesn't mean we all want to be carried away by a knight in shining armor."

"Whatever you say," Becky said. Then, turning to Nick, she continued. "Just call Mark when you're ready for Jessie's number. He's got it on speed dial."

Nick watched as Becky dragged Jessie away toward a large wooden staircase and forced her to stand in the middle of the small group of women gathered there to catch the prized bunch of soon-to-be dead flowers.

The bouquet sailed through the air, heading straight for Jessie. She tried to duck, but at the last second put out her arms so it didn't hit her in the face.

She was the chosen one.

The other women formed a tight knot around her as the groom called out, "All right, guys, it's garter-catching time!"

Time to make his exit, Nick thought. He had no intention of getting anywhere near that garter…even if winning it meant he got to put it on Jessie's thigh.

He headed for the door, casting one last look in Jessie's direction. She was laughing up at Becky, the twinkling fairy lights that lit the room making her smile sparkle even brighter.

Too bad. He sure would have liked to spend the evening getting to know her better.

But they could hook up once they were both back in New York.

He knew where to get her number.

CHAPTER ONE

JESSIE GROWLED WHEN she heard the phone ring. She couldn't possibly reach it from where she sat, huddled under her desk. Not for the first time she cursed the ancient wiring in her office. It shorted out the power strip that kept her laptop juiced at least three times a day, necessitating these little sojourns.

Someday she'd get that fixed. Hopefully someday soon—especially if they kept landing new business.

"Gloria? Can you get that for me?" she shouted, hoping her sister would hear her.

"Got it!" Gloria yelled as she skidded across the slippery wooden floor and dived for the phone.

"Good afternoon, this is Jessie Owens's phone... Yes, she's here. She just needs a minute to get to the phone. Can I tell her who's calling?"

Gloria peered down at Jessie. "A man named Nick is on the phone. He says you two met at Becky's wedding."

Nick? That was a surprise. Given how fast he'd run after she threw herself at him, she hadn't thought she'd ever hear from him again.

Stupid champagne. She knew better than to drink that stuff. All her internal filters disappeared after a couple of glasses.

Finally untangling herself from the mess of cords, she held a hand up to Gloria. "Help me up, would you?"

Gloria pulled, hard and the two women overbalanced, ending up in a pile on the floor.

They looked at each other and burst into giggles.

"Smooth move, ace."

"Right back at ya, grace."

Jessie was still laughing when she spoke into the phone. "Hello, this is Jessie."

"Jessie. It's good to know your laugh sounds just as intoxicating when I'm not hopped up on wedding pheromones," a gravelly voice said.

"I'm surprised you remember how my voice sounded. You sure hightailed it out of there as quickly as you could after we chatted!"

"It wasn't you," he said, his voice low with what she assumed was mock regret. "It was the garter. I didn't want to get anywhere near it."

Jessie laughed again. She could certainly understand that. After she'd caught the bouquet she'd been forced to coo over the flowers with a gaggle of over-hopeful women, then dance with the aging, paunchy bachelor who'd caught the garter.

"I don't blame you. It was a weird scene," she said, leaning back against her desk.

"Weddings usually are. If we'd actually gone back to your room, your friends would have had us married off by morning."

"Nah, they know better. As far as I'm concerned, marriage is a waste of time."

Nick laughed. "I hope you didn't tell Becky that?"

"Of course not. I was my usual supportive self," she answered, picking up the framed picture of the two of them that sat on her desk. "It has been a long time, though. What? Three months? You've been busy, I suppose?"

"Well, you know... I just had to fit a transatlantic move into my schedule, start a new job, and figure out how to save my family's business. Little stuff."

Jessie laughed. "You could have stopped at transatlantic move. That would have been enough for me."

"Yeah, I suppose," he said.

An awkward silence fell and she glanced down at her watch. "Crap," she said before she could choke the word back. "I'm late."

"Late?"

"Yeah, I've got a meeting with a new client and their agency. It's guaranteed to be a hundred kinds of awkward."

"That stinks. As it happens, I'm on my way to an equally awkward meeting even as we speak. I've got to talk my client out of doing something spectacularly stupid—in front of the idiots who are advocating the stupidity."

"That sucks," Jessie said, pulling a navy suit jacket from the hook in her office and dashing out of the brownstone that housed her agency.

"Tell me about it."

"So. What can I do for you?" she said as she clattered down the pavement. "I hate to rush you, but in about three minutes I'll be heading down to the subway—and you know what that does to cell signals."

"Oh. Right. Well, I was wondering if maybe you'd want to attend a charity ball with me tomorrow night. I know it's last-minute, but my father just informed me I have to go and, as I recall, you said you'd love to attend one."

"Will you be picking me up in a pumpkin-shaped carriage?"

"I can if you promise to wear some glass slippers," he replied.

"Touché," she said, pausing at the top of the staircase that led down into the subway. "Okay, you're on! Where should I meet you?"

"Oh, I really will pick you up," he said. "Mark already gave me your address."

"Right. Then I'll see you about eight?"

"Better make it seven."

"Okay. See you then," she said, trying to sound non-chalant.

But inside she was squealing. Going to a ball with the handsome son of a business tycoon? Looking forward to that would certainly get her through this meeting, no matter how badly it went.

Nick looked at his watch, wishing with all his might that his driver would turn off the classical music and step on the gas pedal. Leaning forward, he said, "Bob, can't you go a little faster?"

The bald man turned and made a face at him.

"What? Are you late for a hot date or something?"

"No. Just a meeting with our agency's biggest client."

"The one they brought you back from London to save?" the big man said, one eyebrow raised.

"The one and only."

"Say no more, son. I'll get you there. Buckle up."

As the town car turned off the traffic-jammed street on to a glorified alley Nick quickly did as he was told.

He was more worried about this meeting than he cared to admit. If he could get the cosmetics account back on solid ground it would go a long way toward shoring up the agency's future—and putting an end to the board's threats to sell it.

Silently, Nick cursed his father for selling shares of Thornton & Co. without giving him a chance to buy in. If Nick couldn't get Thornton in the black again his old man would side with those vultures and sell the business he'd promised his grandfather he'd protect—and he wouldn't be able to do anything about it.

Nick thought back to all the times he'd looked for his father in the stands at football games and soccer matches, only to find his grandfather there instead. Remembered all the times his grandfather had been there to help him with his homework when his mom and dad had been missing in action. Hell, his grandfather had been the only one to show up for his high school graduation.

Saving the agency from his father was the least Nick could do to pay him back. Especially since it was the only thing his grandfather had ever asked him to do.

Nick sighed. It was going to take a long time to undo the damage his dad had done. He was going to have to take it one step at a time. First he'd get Goddess back. Then he'd reward himself with a night out with Jessie.

Ever since he'd held her in his arms at the wedding he'd wanted to see more of her. The sound of her laugh was embedded in his brain, tinkling to life at the most inappropriate of times—like when he was out with one of the never-ending stream of society women his mother kept fixing him up with.

He wondered what his mother would say if she saw him with Jessie? Probably something terrible.

There was no way Jessie would win approval from anyone in his family. From what Mark had told him, he knew she didn't have the family ties or social standing that would make her a real person in their eyes. She was a nobody from somewhere in Michigan.

And he already knew what happened when he fell for a "nobody." He got hurt and she got paid to go away.

No need to go through *that* again. Much better to keep things light. Flings were all he allowed himself—and something told him Jessie operated the same way.

"Nick?"

Nick blinked and realized Bob was staring back at him.

"What?"

"We're here."

"Here?"

"Yes. At the site of your hot meeting?"

"Oh. Right," he said, shaking his head to clear it of thoughts of the redhead. "Thanks."

"You want me to wait?"

"No. I don't know how long this will take. Go home to your wife. I'll catch a cab home."

"You sure?"

"Yeah."

"Thanks," Bob said with a grin. "For the record, I'm looking forward to the day you're in charge."

"Me too, Bob. Me too."

With that, he stepped out and headed into the sleek glass building.

Nick waved at the blond-haired receptionist as he strode through the marble foyer.

"Hey, Joan. Are they in the usual spot?"

"They are, indeed," she said. "But don't you have time to chat for a minute?"

"Sorry, babe," he said, giving her his sexiest grin. "Maybe next time."

"All right—fine. But I'll hold you to it!"

He saluted and kept moving through the twelve-foot doors. She was cute, but if he ever had to listen to another one of her stories about Fred, her adorable cat, he might just poke his eyes out.

Still, he'd do whatever he had to to remain a favorite here. Perception was king in advertising, after all.

He looked down at his watch. Seven minutes past three. *Crap.* That meant the meeting had started without him. Still, it wouldn't do to look as if he was in a hurry.

He stopped, took a deep breath, and opened the door, already preparing his apology.

But when he saw what or rather *who* was inside the sleek conference room, the words died in his throat.

"Jessie? What are *you* doing here?"

The redhead looked up from the computer screen she'd been sharing with the elegant gray-haired woman who was his client, a confused look on her face.

"Working. What are *you* doing here, Nick?"

"The same."

Quickly, their client intervened. "I see you two already know each other?" she said. "How convenient."

"Well," Nick said, mind whirling. "We've met—but only socially."

"I didn't even know Nick was in advertising," Jessie added.

"Oh. Well, you're about to get to know each other a lot better," Phyllis said. "Nick—Jessie's company is our new digital partner. I set up this meeting so we could discuss what our strategy will be moving forward."

With that, the pieces of the puzzle clicked. Jessie was in charge of the agency he'd been hoping to dissuade Goddess Cosmetics from using. Suddenly his resolution to do whatever it took to win back every scrap of the Goddess business, even if it meant destroying the other agency, was no longer a challenge he was looking forward to. Instead it was a problem he'd rather avoid.

Still, business had to come first.

Putting his dreams of having a hot affair with Jessie on the back burner, he took his seat at the table.

"Yes. About that… While I'm sure Jessie and her company have plenty of experience in the digital landscape, I don't think it's necessary to direct as much of your marketing budget online as she is recommending," he said, launching into his carefully prepared spiel.

"Let me stop you right there, Nick," Phyllis broke in. "My decision to rely on Roar is not up for discussion. We had Jessie's people do a thorough analysis of the performance of our advertising campaigns over the last few years, and we have decided that something needs to change. The materials your company has delivered are quite frankly stale, and certainly aren't getting the results we need."

"How can you say our work is *stale*? The last campaign we did for you won awards from three different competitions!" Nick said, doing his best not look at the redheaded beauty sitting next to his client.

As long as he didn't have to speak to Jessie he could pretend she was just a troublesome competitor, and not a woman he'd like to see naked.

Phyllis sighed and fiddled with her pen. "Yes, yes, that's true. But you used the same old tired tactics. TV, radio, magazine ads… We don't care what the advertising community thinks. We care what our *customers* think. And you're not reaching them. To do that you've got to be on the internet. You've got to speak to them on those virtual networks—like Jessie, here, does."

Jessie cleared her throat and glanced up for the first time since he'd sat down, discomfort shining in her blue eyes. "The term is *social* networks, Phyl," she said. "And, yes, you *do* have to be there. Our research tells us—"

"I don't care what your research says," Nick broke in. "My agency has been handling Goddess' advertising for fifty-six years. I think we know what your customers want, Phyllis."

"You're wrong," Jessie said.

Pushing a button on her laptop, she got out of her chair and went to stand where she could point at the chart that had appeared on the projector screen.

"See this red line?" she asked, looking directly at him, challenge vibrating in every line of her body.

"Of course I do," he answered, trying not to notice how well she filled out the lime-green sheath she was wearing.

"That represents the sales figures for the Goddess line over the last three years. As you can see, they've gone down twelve quarters in a row."

"That's not our fault—" he started.

"I wasn't finished," she snapped. A new slide replaced the old—this one a bar graph.

"This slide shows us how sales have been affected by advertising efforts. As you can see, profits actually went *down* after the launch of the last campaign—and stayed there. Obviously something isn't working."

Nick was silent for a moment. She had a point. He knew she did. But since he'd only gotten control of the Goddess account two months ago those numbers didn't reflect what *his* team was capable of.

"I am aware of that. But I've hired a new creative team and we're working on materials that will mitigate the problem." He turned his attention to Phyllis. "Give us three months and I promise you you'll see a big difference. The things we're working on are like nothing you've ever seen before."

"Good, good…I'm glad to hear it," Phyllis said, a pained smile on her face. "But I don't have three months to wait. We're launching a new product line in six weeks, and I need a big campaign to introduce it to the marketplace."

Nick's heart plummeted. "New product line? Well. That's interesting." Thinking fast, he continued, "That's not much time, but I'm sure my team can handle it. We'll have to work night and day, but I am confident we can have some concepts for you to review within the week."

"No need, no need. Jessie already has it figured out. Her team has come up with a dynamite campaign."

Nick glanced her way, his blood boiling. She had just made his life—*and* his plan to get the agency back on track—a great deal more difficult. Taking a deep breath, he said, "Okay—good. You've got digital handled. But we'll still need to get the print ads going, and TV, and probably some direct mail. You can't launch a product without investing in traditional advertising."

"All in good time," his client said, leather creaking as she leaned back in her chair. "But there's no need to rush. We're going to put our entire marketing budget in the digital space for the launch. Then, after we've gotten a foothold there, you guys can do your stuff."

Nick swallowed, unable to believe what he was hearing. "So you don't want Thornton involved in the launch at all?"

"I think what she's saying is that Roar is in charge and you should follow our lead," Jessie said, squirming in her chair.

"You're trusting Roar with this? No offense, but I think that's a huge mistake."

"Be that as it may, Jessie's got the helm on this one," Phyllis said, getting up from her chair. "Make sure whatever materials you eventually present are in line with what she's doing. And now, if you'll excuse me, I need to move on to my next meeting. I'm sure you two have plenty to talk about, so feel free to stay as long as you like."

And with that she was gone.

Nick stared at his adversary, wishing she wasn't so damn attractive. And that his hands didn't itch to hold her.

Channeling the haughty air that was his birthright as a fourth generation advertising executive, he looked calmly across the table.

"Do you have *any* idea what you've gotten yourself into?"

Jessie blinked. How dared he address her like some sort of troublesome child?

He'd been driving her crazy since the second he walked in. That haughty sneer hadn't left his face for more than two seconds. He certainly wasn't acting anything *like* the man she met at Becky's wedding.

And now he questioned her abilities?

"I think I just got a hold of a branch on your money tree—that's what I think. And you don't like me shaking it."

He snorted.

"Don't kid yourself. This is a drop in the bucket for my agency. Besides, Phyllis will wise up and come running back in no time. You don't have what it takes to keep an account like this happy."

Jessie stalked across the room until she stood directly in front of him.

"How do you know what I can handle? You don't know anything about me."

"I know I've never heard of an agency called Roar," he said, leaning back in his chair with his arms behind his head, one side of his mouth curling up in a sneer. "And, since I pride myself on being familiar with every agency worth knowing in this city, I'm guessing you haven't done much worth talking about."

For the first time Jessie understood the expression "seeing red." It was all she could do not to reach up and strangle him with his tie. But since getting mad was probably exactly what he wanted her to do, she did the opposite. Putting her hands behind her, she hopped up on the giant mahogany table and crossed her legs, making sure he got an eyeful of thigh.

Nick's eyes widened and he swallowed loudly, his body giving away his sudden interest.

"That's a very interesting theory," she said. "But I think if you ask around you'll find plenty of people talking about us. Perhaps you're just out of touch? Like your agency."

Nick looked at her with a predatory gaze and it was her turn to swallow loudly. Even knowing he was now the competition, a part of her still wanted him.

"Careful, Jessie. I might be 'out of touch,' as you say, but I could still crush you and your little agency without breaking a sweat."

"I'd like to see you try."

"Don't tempt me," he growled.

She slowly slid down off her perch, letting her skirt ride up in the process, and watched as he caught a ragged breath.

"Oh, I'm very good at tempting men. In fact there's only one thing I do better," she said as she sauntered back to her laptop.

"Which is…?"

She threw him a smile as she snapped the lid shut. "Kicking their butts with my advertising."

She quickly stowed the computer in her bag, anxious to get away before her disappointment had a chance to catch up with her. It was just her luck that Prince Charming had turned out to be King of the Schmucks.

But when she turned to leave she found her way blocked by a solid wall of muscle. Damn, she hadn't remembered he was so tall…or so deliciously built.

She tried to move past without touching him. "Excuse me. You're in my way."

"We haven't finished our conversation. About what you're getting into."

She looked up at him, a retort on the tip of her tongue, but when he caught her gaze the words died in her throat. His eyes burned into hers, silently communicating an encyclopedia's worth of knowledge about want and need and straight-up danger.

She stared at him helplessly, trying to think of something that wasn't, *Kiss me now, you hot, sexy—*

"Getting into?" she asked, trying unsuccessfully to keep the squeak from her voice.

"Yes. You're in the big league now. The stakes are bigger. The sharks are hungrier. You sure you're up for the challenge?"

Forcing herself to step back, she swallowed, then answered, "I've never been more ready for anything in my life."

He opened his mouth to answer, but before he could Phyllis bustled in.

"Oh, good, you two are still here," she said, oblivious to the mood in the room. "As Nick already knows, Goddess is sponsoring a charity ball tomorrow. Two seats have just opened up at my table and I'd like you to take them."

"I'd be happy to take them off your hands," Jessie said quickly. "I'm sure I can find someone to come with me."

"No, you don't understand," Phyllis said. "I want you to attend the ball together. The higher-ups are worried about the direction we're taking our advertising in. The two of you presenting a united front would go a long way toward allaying their fears."

Jessie looked at Nick, unsure of what to say. While going to a ball with him had seemed like a dream come true just a couple of hours ago, now it seemed nightmare-worthy.

"I'd be happy to accompany Jessie to the ball," Nick said with a smooth smile. "After a couple of glasses of champagne she might tell me the secrets of her success."

Jessie conjured up a hollow laugh. "Not likely, but it'll be fun to see you try and get them out of me!"

Phyllis nodded. "Great. It's all set, then. I'll see you two tomorrow…at the ball!"

"Looking forward to it," Jessie said, crossing her fingers behind her back.

After Phyllis exited, Nick turned to her with a grim smile. "Pick you up at seven?"

She shook her head. "No. I'll meet you there."

"Bad idea. People will notice if we don't arrive together."

Jessie's temper flared. How dared he tell her what to do? "I'm not sure I care."

Nick scowled. "Well, I do. Unlike you, I'm willing to do

whatever it takes to keep my client happy. And she wants us to put up a united front. So I'll pick you up at seven."

Then he turned on his heel and left, not waiting for her reply.

Jessie's heart pounded and the blood roared in her veins. How dared he be so presumptuous? So controlling? He was turning out to be everything she hated about corporate advertising.

Stupid man. She hoped he was feeling good about his little victory—there was no way he was going to get another one.

CHAPTER TWO

NICK SIGHED. HE'D JUST spent three hours going through the advertising materials for the Goddess account, hoping to see a spark of brilliance that he'd overlooked before, but Phyllis was right. They were old. Tired. Stale. There wasn't a single mention of social media, or online videos, or anything interactive at all.

Thornton had missed the digital advertising boat entirely. It was no wonder that Roar had been able to wow Phyllis so easily. His agency hadn't even tried.

He put his feet up on the giant wooden desk he'd been given and leaned back in his chair, looking for answers on the ceiling. He knew how to turn Thornton & Co. around. He just had to convince his father to listen to him.

Right on cue, his father barged in, storming through the door with his usual attitude of barely contained rage.

"Thanks for knocking, Dad," he said, hoping his father would notice the sarcasm dripping from his voice.

"What? Are you hiding a girl in here or something?"

"Of course not. But—"

"But nothing. I need to talk to you—and I'm not about to let that secretary of yours come up with an excuse to keep me out again.

"She prefers to be called my assistant."

"Whatever. I don't want to talk about the woman you've got taking your calls. We need to discuss the lion woman."

"Lion?" Nick asked, genuinely confused.

"Yes. The gal who runs the web thing."

"Oh. You mean Jessie. Her agency is called Roar."

His father snorted. "And if *that's* not a ridiculous name for an agency I don't know what is. You got any Scotch in here?"

"No. I'm not in the habit of drinking in the office."

"More's the pity," his father said, before settling in one of the ancient burgundy leather armchairs Nick had inherited when he took over this office. "Your generation has taken all the fun out of advertising. I remember when—"

"Dad. I don't have time for a trip down Memory Lane right now. I'm trying to figure out how to save our agency."

"Yes. That's what I wanted to discuss with you. First of all, you need to eliminate Roar from the picture."

"Obviously that would be ideal, but we don't have the resources to do what she does. If you had invested in digital when I told you to we wouldn't be in this situation," Nick said, trying not to let his temper get the best of him.

His father waved his hand. "Let's not start that again. I brought you back because you said you wanted to fix things—not rehash the past."

Nick motioned toward the piles of spreadsheets and glossy ads in front of him. "That's what I'm trying to do."

"You're not going to find the answer in paperwork. You should be buttering Phyllis up—getting her to fall for the good ol' Thornton charm. I know you've got it in you."

Nick couldn't stop the roll of his eyes. "Phyllis is smarter than that. Besides, she's been happily married for a million years."

"True. But she's still a woman." His father folded his hands behind his head and looked up at the ceiling, as if a slideshow was playing there. "There's not a woman in the world who doesn't want to feel wanted by a handsome man. Why, I can't tell you how many times I've closed a deal because of—"

"Dad!" Nick shouted.

He sat up straight again. "What?"

It took everything he had not to grab a roll of duct tape and shut his father's mouth for him. "I don't want to hear about your glory days. I want to talk about how we can set this agency up to start winning again—and shut down the buyout bid."

His father slumped back in his chair and sighed. "All right. Fine. Shoot."

Nick took a deep breath. He had to remain calm if he wanted his father to listen to him. "We need to go digital. *Now.* I need you to give me free rein to set up an online advertising division. I'll invest in the latest equipment. Steal all the best people from the already established agencies. And then I'll have them create spec work for all our current clients. Before you know it we'll have a giant new revenue stream without having to go through a single pitch."

"And how does that help us with our current problem?"

"It ensures that we never lose another piece of business to an upstart like Roar."

His father nodded. "All right. I'll think about it. In the meantime I want you to get the Goddess launch back in our court."

"I plan to—but I'll need to prove to them we can handle their digital needs first."

His father slammed a fist into the arm of his chair. "You don't have to *prove* anything. Just give 'em a little theater. Come up with a great campaign idea, put together a slick presentation, and *bam!* Roar is history."

"It's not going to be that easy to beat Roar. Phyllis loves Jessie."

"You think so?" he asked, one eyebrow raised.

"I *know* so. Phyllis has commanded us to appear at the charity ball together. She wants us to present a united front to make the higher-ups feel better."

"And you agreed?"

Nick sighed. "At this point I'm willing to do just about anything to keep Phyllis happy."

His father nodded as he got up to leave. "Just make sure you keep it about business. It wouldn't do to get involved with this harpy."

"I wouldn't dream of it."

That was a lie. He'd been dreaming about what she'd look like with her clothes off quite a bit.

For now that was off the table. But after he'd beaten Roar he had every intention of getting her naked.

Jessie looked at herself in the dressing room mirror, smoothing her hands over the emerald-green silk of the form-fitting evening gown she was wearing.

"I don't know, Gloria. It's a little too…"

"Too what? Elegant? Classy? Gorgeous?" snorted the long-legged brunette from her seat on the floor.

"I was going to say too much. It isn't *me*."

"Oh, Jessie. You're going to a black tie gala. That sequined bandage you usually pass off as formal attire isn't going to work this time."

"Maybe we should keep looking."

"No. No, we shouldn't. You've already tried on every other dress in your size in the store," Gloria said, pointing at the towering stack of evening gowns that was draped over the dressing room's upholstered chair.

"You're sure?"

"I'm sure."

Jessie sighed as she twisted her hair up into a loose bun and stared at her reflection. She knew her sister was right, but she felt like a little girl playing dress-up in her mother's clothes. The elegant, polished woman staring back at her from the mirror was a stranger to her.

"Maybe I shouldn't go at all. I could just call Phyllis and tell her something came up."

"What's going on, Jessie?" her sister asked, crossing the small room to stand in front of her. "This isn't like you. Are you scared?"

"No, not scared. Just intimidated."

"Why? Your agency—the agency *we* started less than two years ago—has been chosen to launch a huge make-up line. You've been asked to attend one of the year's most prestigious charity balls as the guest of that same make-up line. And you'll be sitting right next to someone from New York's biggest and oldest ad agency—the agency that *you* showed up and outdid. This is your moment to shine!"

"But what if I say or do something stupid and completely blow it? I'm afraid they'll know I don't belong there the minute I open my mouth."

"You're going to be sitting with a bunch of aging white guys, wearing a gorgeous dress and looking like a million bucks. You could speak in pig Latin all night and no one would blink an eye."

Jessie grinned, realizing her sister was right. Powerful men always seemed to want her. "Should I see if I can get Roar a sugar daddy?"

"Roar doesn't need one. We've got you. But no one would blame you if you wanted to get one for yourself!"

"Nah. I don't want to get chained down to anyone—let alone some ancient guy—even if he comes with designer shoes and private yachts."

"What about the hot young advertising executive who's escorting you?"

Nick. As soon as his name crossed her mind a confusing mix of rage and lust clouded her thoughts. She remembered the way he'd sneered at her after he'd found out it was her agency that had stolen his business. And how he'd tried to use his size to intimidate her. She wouldn't go near him with a ten-foot pole.

"Thanks, but no thanks. His ego would take up too much of the bed."

Gloria squeezed her shoulder. "All right—whatever, sis. Just don't let him get to you. You're worth ten of him."

Jessie nodded, feeling better after the pep talk.

"Thanks, Gloria," she said, moving in for a hug.

Gloria squeaked and backed out of her reach. "No hugging while you're wearing that dress—you might wrinkle it. Pretend you're one of those frozen heiress types. Air kisses only!"

"Right. Okay. Help me out of this, will you? I don't want to play the frozen princess until I have to."

"We're here, boss."

Nick started. "Already? That was fast."

"Not really." Bob snorted. "You were just lost in space. I don't think you blinked once the whole way here."

Nick frowned. "Just trying to figure out how to handle the evening. I'm used to escorting shallow debutantes— not my biggest competitor."

"Just treat her like you would any other woman. Open doors, pull out her chair and turn on the charm. She'll be a puddle at your feet in no time."

Nick tried to imagine Jessie melting, but the image that came to mind was of *her* vaporizing *him*. "I don't know about that. This one's a fighter."

"You won't know until you try. Go."

"You're right. As usual."

Besides, he had no choice. Phyllis was expecting them in less than an hour. Nick took a deep breath and looked at his surroundings. The neighborhood of elegant but boring brownstones didn't look like the kind of place Jessie would call home.

He motioned toward the one they were parked in front of. "Are you sure this is the right address?"

"That one's not. But *that* one is," Bob said, pointing across the street.

Nick laughed out loud as he took in the fuchsia-painted exterior of the house Bob was pointing at. "Of course it is."

He got out of the limo and walked up the brightly tiled mosaic path that led to the front door, still grinning. He pushed the doorbell and was unsurprised to hear a lion roaring in response inside the house.

Seconds later a fresh-faced brunette opened the door. "You must be Nick," she said.

"The one and only. And you are…?"

"Gloria. Jessie's sister and office manager. Come on in. She'll be down in a second."

Nick stepped inside and was surprised to find himself in a lobby environment, complete with receptionist's desk and pink and black polka-dotted armchairs.

"You guys run Roar out of here?"

"Yep. The ground floor and basement are for the business. Jessie and I live on the top two floors."

"I just assumed it was a bigger operation."

The woman shrugged. "It's bigger than it used to be. There's fifteen of us now. When Jessie and I started it was just the two of us."

"And when was that?

"A little over a year ago. Can I get you some water or something?"

He shook his head, trying to wrap his brain around the fact that his competition was so inexperienced. How had they managed to snag an account like Goddess?

"Okay, then. Make yourself comfortable. She'll be down in a minute."

He sank into one of the plush chairs, shaking his head at the absurdity of it all. But before he had a chance to get too comfortable he heard the clacking of high heels crossing the hardwood floor.

He looked up and felt all the breath leave his body.

Jessie was a vision of sparkling emerald and fiery red. Her dress clung to her curves in all the right places and her hair tumbled loose around her bare shoulders.

"Wow."

She smiled grimly. "I'll interpret that as, *You clean up well, Jessie*."

Nick rose to his feet. "That you do. You look beautiful."

She stepped back and gave him a once-over, her eyes slowly roaming over his body.

"You're not looking too shabby either. I think you'll do."

"Good to know."

An awkward silence fell as they stared at each other, neither wanting to make the next move.

It didn't bode well for the evening.

Nick sighed, realizing he was going to have to be the one to break the silence if they were ever going to make it out through the door.

"All right, so obviously neither one of us wants to be here. But we're supposed to be supporting Phyllis, so we need to do our best to look like we're pleased with the way things are going."

Jessie raised an eyebrow. "So you're going to pretend to be *happy* about losing out on the Natural Goddess launch?"

Nick took a deep breath. He would *not* let her get to him. "Well, I don't know if I can channel 'happy,' but I think I can do collegial."

She looked at him silently for a moment, her expression still as stone.

"I don't know that I can."

He raised an eyebrow. "Oh, really? That's certainly good for me."

She crossed her arms around her chest. "What do you mean?"

"Most of the people in the room at this ball are going to

hate each other. But they're perfectly capable of pretending to be best buddies when the situation calls for it. If you can't play the game, your agency is doomed to fail."

Jessie scowled. "Of course I can play the game. I'd just rather not play it with *you*."

Nick stood to leave. Although Jessie looked damned sexy when she was angry, his life would certainly be easier if she wasn't there. "Fine. I'll give Phyllis your regrets. Don't worry. I'll make sure they don't miss you."

"God, you're a bastard."

Nick forced his lips into a smile, trying to ignore the sting her words caused. He liked to think his father was the only devil in the Thornton family. "Indeed I am. It's good for business. Enjoy your evening." And he reached for the doorknob.

"Wait."

He turned back to face her. "Yes?"

"I'll come." She shrugged on her wrap. "And I'll do my best to be cordial."

He wasn't sure whether he should be disappointed or glad at her change in attitude. "May I ask why?"

"Because I'm not going to let you beat me that easily. I'm willing to do whatever it takes to keep this business."

Nick stepped close, purposely invading her personal space. "Even if it means getting closer to me?"

Heat flashed across her face, but she quickly hid it and stepped back. "Not *that* close."

They would just have to see about that.

"Message received," he said out loud, and held out his arm for her to take. "Shall we go?"

"Yes, indeed." She put her hand delicately on his forearm.

"Great."

He shook his head slightly as they set off down the walkway. One thing was for sure—with Jessie on his arm, the evening would be anything but boring.

Jessie tried not to be impressed when she saw the limo that waited at the curb. But when his driver got out to hold the door open for her, her jaw dropped. They were definitely not in Kansas anymore.

"Nice ride," she said after he'd slid in next to her.

"It is," Nick answered. "But it's not my favorite."

"How many cars do you have?"

"Well, the agency has six limos that are kept for the use of the family. This is one of those. Left to my own devices, though, I prefer to ride my motorcycle."

"I wouldn't have pegged you for a biker."

"And I wouldn't have pegged *you* as a cold-hearted boardroom ball-buster," he answered. "But you are."

That stung, but Jessie tried not to show it. The last thing she wanted was to turn into another "business first, last and always" power-monger.

"I'm not cold-hearted. Just determined. It's time the ad world got a shot of estrogen, but you guys aren't going to make room for female-owned shops like mine if we ask politely."

Nick smiled. "Actually, I would have been more than happy to work with you. I just don't appreciate you stealing one of my biggest clients."

Jessie took a deep breath to calm her temper, but as his spicy scent hit her nostrils she wished she hadn't. For a moment her inner lioness threatened to take over. And all *she* wanted to do was crawl into Nick's lap and find out how he tasted.

But that was definitely not going to happen.

Jessie shook her head to clear it. "We're supposed to be being collegial tonight, remember? That means no comments like that. Tell me about this ball we're going to instead."

Nick shrugged. "What do you want to know? As far as I'm concerned it's just another boring charity gala in another fancy hotel ballroom, populated by a bunch of socialites with the emotional depth of a pancake. If you've been to one, you've been to them all."

"Yes, but I've never been to one. Tell me what to expect."

Just then the car stopped. "We've arrived," the chauffeur said.

"Too late." Nick slid across the seat until his thigh pressed against hers. "But there's really only one thing you need to know."

Jessie swallowed, her mouth suddenly dry. "What's that?"

"You're going to be the most beautiful woman in the room."

That was so far away from what she'd expected to hear she wasn't sure she'd heard correctly.

"What did you say?"

"You heard me. Don't make me repeat myself."

The heat in his sapphire gaze pinned her to the spot. He bent his head down toward hers and her pulse jumped in response. He hovered centimeters away, his eyes still locked on hers.

"I want you more than I've wanted anything in a very long time," he said. "But if you get in my way I'll still crush you like a bug."

She gasped, outraged. But before she could think of a suitably cutting retort the driver opened the door.

His face turned into a blank mask as he sat up straight.

"Let's get this over with," he muttered.

She slid out of the car, gulping the fresh, non-Nick-scented air to clear her head. Obviously he knew the effect he had on her and wasn't afraid to use it. But now that she knew he intended to play that game, he wouldn't be able to surprise her again.

This was business. And he was the enemy. It wouldn't do to forget that, even if they were playing nice for the evening.

Seconds later, Nick appeared beside her.

"Ready?"

"As I'll ever be."

He nodded and set off up the marble stairs, not looking to see if she was following. She did her best to keep up, but the five-inch stilettos she was wearing made it difficult. At the door he turned, and looked momentarily chagrined when he saw her still picking her way up.

"Sorry about that. I seem to have forgotten my manners this evening."

"I suppose that's to be expected when you're forced to play escort to a woman you don't even like," she said, trying to make light of the situation.

Nick smiled, purposely letting his gaze drift down to her cleavage. "I like you fine. In fact, if you agree to give up the Goddess account, I'll make sure we have a lovely evening."

Jessie pulled her wrap more tightly around her shoulders. "Not a chance, bud."

He shrugged. "All right, then. I'll escort you to the table and then you're on your own."

"Fine by me," she said shortly.

He held the door open, sweeping his arm out with false gallantry. "After you."

Seeing the mockery in his eyes, she straightened her spine, held her head high, and stepped through into the ballroom beyond.

She didn't need him, no matter how sexy he was. She had all of New York's advertising elite waiting to be wrapped around her little finger.

CHAPTER THREE

"NICK! JESSIE! THANK GOODNESS!" Phyllis said as they approached the table. "I thought that perhaps you weren't coming!"

Jessie forced herself to smile as Nick gave the plump older woman's matronly purple dress an appreciative glance.

"I wouldn't have missed the chance to see you looking this beautiful for the world. You *will* do me the honor of dancing with me this evening, won't you?"

"Oh, Nick. Always such a flirt," Phyllis said.

Realizing that she needed to make her presence known before Nick stole the show, Jessie shouldered her way in to their cozy circle. "I've never met an ad man who wasn't. But Nick is a master!"

"You're certainly right about that," Phyllis said. "Thank you, you two, for doing this. I know it's an awkward situation I've put you into."

Jessie waved her comment away. "No problem. It sounds like we're going to be working very closely in the future. Might as well present a solid front now!"

"Indeed," Nick added. "The only thing that matters is that your company is successful. We won't let our egos get in the way of that."

"Good, good… Jessie, let me introduce you around. There are some people here you need to meet. Nick, you'll come with us, won't you?"

After the introductions were over Nick excused himself and Jessie found herself sitting alone at the table. Picking up her long-neglected glass of champagne, she took a good look at her surroundings. She couldn't believe how many of the women were wearing the kind of designer gowns she'd only seen in fashion magazines. They were all thorough-bred-thin, their brittle expressions weighed down by heavy make-up. Circulating around them were dozens of self-important businessmen, their wealth apparent in the size of their Rolexes and the youth of the women on their arms.

She didn't belong here. *At all.*

Even the music was wrong. There was a band playing, but the songs they played were old and slow. Nothing like the dance music that blared in the clubs she liked.

She gulped down the last of the bubbly liquid and opened her black satin clutch to peek at the clock on her phone. Only an hour had passed. She definitely couldn't leave yet. But perhaps she could find herself another drink.

Just as she was about to push away from the table a suave gray-haired man approached.

"Is anyone sitting here?"

"You are," she said, hoping she looked less intimidated than she felt.

"Great." He pulled out the chair. "I'm Brad Thornton."

She knew she should know that name, but her mind was drawing a blank.

"It's nice to meet you, Brad. I'm…"

"Jessie Owens—the digital marketing sensation. I know."

"How did you…?"

He smiled. "I know everything that goes on in this town. Especially when it concerns one of my clients."

Everything fell into place. She looked at her empty glass, wishing she could have a quick sip of champagne to settle her nerves.

"Oh, so you're Nick's…?"

"Father. And, for at least a little while longer, the head of Thornton & Co."

Crap. This was one conversation she wasn't prepared for. "I've always admired your agency's work," she said, grabbing at conversational straws.

He relaxed back into his seat. "I wish I could say the same about yours, but I don't have any idea what you've done."

Jessie wondered if she should be insulted by his ignorance. Either way, the man deserved to be taken down a peg or two. "Well, you will soon enough! We're in charge of the launch for the Natural Goddess line—as I'm sure your son told you."

His face darkened. "I know. And I am *not* thrilled. But we *have* been resting on our laurels a bit. It was about time for someone like you to come along and shake us up."

Jessie let out a breath she hadn't realized she'd been holding. "You're not angry?"

His mouth twisted up into a grim smile. "Oh, I'm angry, all right. But not at you. My son will answer for this one."

"What is it that I'm answering for?" a familiar voice growled from behind them.

The elder Thornton looked up. "Ah, Nick. We were just talking about how you let the Natural Goddess launch slip through your fingers."

Nick pulled out a chair and sat down, his face a polite mask. "Really? Did you also happen to tell her that I've only just returned from our London office? And that Goddess Cosmetics has only been mine for two and a half months? Or were you about to place the blame for three years of failure at my door?"

"There's no blame being placed here, Nick. Only the foundation for a new partnership."

As the two men eyed each other Jessie found herself becoming more and more uncomfortable.

"Well, it seems as if you two could use a little time alone to work things out. If you'll excuse me...?" she said, rising to go.

Nick's hand clamped around her wrist. "Don't leave. I was just about to ask you to dance."

Well, *that* was a switch. "You were?"

"Yes. Will you?"

Despite the alarm bells ringing in her brain, Jessie nodded. "Of course. We're presenting a solid front, right?"

"Right."

"It was nice to meet you, Brad," she said, ignoring the pressure Nick was placing on her hand.

"Likewise. I look forward to having many more conversations with you."

She nodded and let Nick lead her on to the dance floor.

Nick led Jessie into the center of the dancing throng before pulling her into his arms. The band had begun a slow waltz and his body automatically began to move to the music, even though his temper was raging. If it hadn't been for his father's inability to keep up with the times they wouldn't be in this situation in the first place.

"What was that about?" Jessie asked.

Nick looked down at the gorgeous redhead in his arms and tried to think of an answer that wouldn't give anything away. The last thing he needed was for her to get wind of the company's financial troubles. If Phyllis heard about it she'd have even less faith in their abilities.

"Nick?"

He blinked. *Oh. Right.* She was waiting for an answer.

"I'm sorry—what was the question again?"

She rolled her eyes. "What was that thing with your father all about? For a minute there I thought you might punch him."

"Oh, just the usual family drama. My father brings out

the best in me, if you know what I mean," he said, trying to keep the snarl out of his voice.

"And my existence brings out the best in you both, apparently?"

Nick managed a smile. "Neither one of us is used to being bested—especially not by someone as sexy as you. It stings the pride a bit."

"Ah, so you're admitting to being beaten?" she asked, raising an eyebrow.

"We lost a battle, but I'm confident we'll win the war."

Jessie took a deep breath and he could see the temper sparking in her eyes. But instead of rising to the bait she shook her head and smiled.

"I think we'd better change the subject before our cover is blown, don't you?"

"You're right."

For a moment they were silent as they twirled around the room.

"You're quite the dancer—even when you're angry," Jessie finally said.

Looking down at her, he felt something shift inside. His anger dissipated, only to be replaced by a different kind of heat. God, but she was gorgeous. And fun. If circumstances were different they could have a seriously good time together.

"If you're going to do something there's no sense in half-assing it."

He spun her out for a twirl, pulled her back in and swept her down into a dip, just as he had at Becky's wedding.

With his face inches from hers, he said, "I pride myself on doing things right."

Jessie's face flushed and he could see the desire he was feeling reflected back in her eyes.

"I'll just bet you do."

Nick became all too aware of how well her lithe body

fit in his arms, and of the silk-clad thigh currently locked between his legs.

Quickly, he set her on her feet. "Man, it's hot in here. I'm going to get some air," he said, motioning toward the doors open to the rooftop deck.

"That sounds like a fabulous idea."

Moments later they were standing in the chilly night air, looking over the deck's railing, the lights of the city sparkling below and around them.

The tension Nick hadn't even known he was feeling evaporated into the night. "I don't think I'll ever get tired of the way New York looks at night."

"Me neither. The first time I came here my mom took me up to the top of the Empire State Building at night and said, 'See those lights? Fairies live in every sparkle. There are millions of them, all around us. New York is the most magical city in the world.'"

"Fairies, huh? I never thought of that."

Jessie looked at him with a sad smile. "Most people wouldn't. But my mom saw things other people didn't."

"Past tense?"

"Yeah. She died when I was sixteen," Jessie said, hunching in on herself.

She looked so vulnerable Nick wished he could put his arm around her. "I'm sorry," he said instead. "That's a rough age to lose a parent."

"Yes. It is. But it taught me an important lesson."

"What's that?"

She spread her arms wide. "To live. *Really* live—not just go through the motions. I don't want to be on my deathbed thinking about all the things I wish I'd done, you know? That's a terrible way to spend your last days."

"Well, from the little I know of you, I'd say you're doing a pretty good job so far."

She turned away from the railing and looked up at him, her eyes searching his.

"What about you?"

"What about me?"

"Are *you* really living?"

"I'd like to think so."

She waved her hands toward the crowded ballroom. "Does this make you happy?"

"I thought I'd made my position on charity balls pretty clear? They're a giant bore. This side of New York life is not my thing."

"Then let's get out of here," she said, grabbing his arm and tugging. "I'll show you how much more fun *my* New York is."

Nick blinked. That was a switch. "Together? But I thought you couldn't stand me?"

"I can't stand Nicholas Thornton, advertising bigwig. But Nick the *guy* is growing on me. How about we forget about our real lives and pretend to be two regular people out on a Saturday night for a few hours?"

The suspicious part of him wondered if she was playing some sort of game—trying to get a competitive advantage. But he decided to play it cool. "That's definitely a change in attitude. Are you always this impulsive?"

She shrugged her shoulders. "Usually. It makes life way more exciting when you go with your gut. So what do you say?"

Nick was silent for a minute. Rationally, he knew he should say no and head back inside to network and flatter. But he really wanted to get to know this fascinating woman better. Besides, if they spent more time together he might discover something that would help him get the Goddess account back.

"All right. Let's go. Where are we going?"

"I don't know…" She shrugged. "Somewhere."

"Somewhere it is," he said, and gave her his hand. "Lead the way!"

Jessie hummed as she weaved down the familiar set of backstreets and alleyways, still holding Nick's hand. The evening had become pretty surreal. One minute she'd been trying to think of a graceful way to make an exit. The next she'd heard herself inviting him to come with her.

It was the conversation about her mom that had done it. Whenever she let herself remember how abruptly her mom had died she found herself doing something reckless. Something that made her feel alive. Something she usually regretted later.

"Are we there yet?" Nick asked, breaking into her reverie.

Jessie blinked and looked around her. Then she nodded and pointed at the faded sign ahead. "Yep. Welcome to the first stop on your tour of Jessie's New York."

"Tina's Thrift Shop?"

"Yep. We have to change before we head to our next venue."

Nick stopped cold. "You're kidding?"

"Nope. What are you? Chicken?"

Nick's expression heated as he played with a tendril of her hair. "Of course not. But you didn't have to drag me all the way down here to get me out of my clothes. You could've just asked. I would have happily obliged."

Jessie ignored the tingles his words set off in her thighs. "Well, I *do* plan on getting you hot and sweaty tonight. But I have no interest in what you're hiding beneath that monkey suit."

"All right—have it your way," he said. "But mine would be more fun. Let's go."

The bell tinkled as she led him inside.

"Jessie, what a nice surprise," a disembodied voice called.

"I need your help finding some eighties gear!" Jessie called back.

Suddenly a small woman popped her head out from around a clothing rack and whistled.

"*Wowsa*. Looking good, girlie."

Jessie twirled. "I know—don't I? Too good. And so does he. Help us out, would ya?"

After giving Nick a quick once-over, she nodded. "Of course. Come with me."

Jessie grinned and followed her to the back of the store, where Tina was already digging through piles.

"How about one of these?" the woman asked, holding up a lime green mini-dress and a black net shirt.

Jessie threw an evil smile in Nick's direction. "Yep, those would be perfect for him."

His carefully impassive expression cracked. "You're kidding. I…"

"Relax—I wouldn't do that to you." Jessie giggled, enjoying his discomfort. "However, I *do* think you should get these," she said, throwing the red parachute silk pants she'd found at him.

"You're not serious?"

"Just try them on. Please?"

His smile widened and his expression grew predatory. "Fine. I'll put them on. On one condition."

"Which is…?"

"You help me."

Oh, no. She didn't need to be anywhere in the vicinity when his clothes came off. That crossed the line from recklessness to insanity. "We can't go in the dressing room together," she blurted. "Tina wouldn't allow it."

"Oh, sure you can, honey," Tina called. "You're going to need someone to help you get that dress off anyway."

"See? It's fine." He grinned at her. "What are you…
chicken?"

Damn. He had her. She couldn't stand to be called a
coward. "Of course not. Lead the way."

A few minutes later she was still kicking herself as
he drew his shirt over his head. As hard as she tried she
couldn't bite back the gasp that worked its way up her throat
when she saw the tight muscles of his chest gleaming in
the fluorescent light.

"Like what you see?"

She cleared her throat. "*Meh*. I've seen better," she lied.
In reality, she wanted nothing more than to press herself
against him and kiss every muscled inch of his torso.

"Oh, really?"

"Of course. This is New York, after all. Handsome men
are a dime a dozen. In fact, you should probably just get
dressed now."

"Fine. If that's the way you want to play it," he said,
reaching behind her to grab the black silk T she'd found
him.

She sighed quietly as the fabric hid his magnificent pecs
from view.

Dressed again, he stood staring silently at her.

"What?"

His eyes glowed with challenge. "I showed you mine.
Time to show me yours."

He was right. Telling herself it was no different than letting a man see her in her swimsuit, she nodded.

"Fine. Can you help me…?" She motioned to the zipper
that ran down the back of her dress. "I can't reach."

"I'd be happy to," he growled.

She closed her eyes and breathed deep, trying to tell herself not to feel anything as his knuckles brushed against

her skin. But as he slowly tugged the zipper down she felt herself trembling, her body flooding with heat. Who knew such a simple act could be so erotic?

At long last he unzipped the last teeth and her dress gaped open. She shimmied out of it and with a deep breath, turned to face him.

"Ta-dah!" she said, throwing in some jazz hands.

His eyes devoured her body, seeming to see right through the black velvet strapless bra and lacy thong that were all she was wearing. The hunger in his eyes when he returned his gaze to her face took her breath away.

"You're beautiful," he said, his voice barely more than a growl.

"Yes, but there are plenty of beautiful women in New York," she said, still striving for nonchalance.

"Not as beautiful as you," he said, moving toward her.

Jessie knew she should back up, or look away—or something. But her feet rooted her to the spot. She wanted him to touch her so very badly...

"How's everything going in there?" Tina called—and just like that the moment passed.

Jessie threw the Spandex dress over her head. "Perfect," she said as she pulled it down over her butt, not daring to look at Nick. "We're going to rock this thing."

"Well, let me see 'em!" called Tina.

Jessie glanced up at Nick, who nodded, seemingly unruffled.

Throwing open the dressing room curtain, she said, "What do you think?"

Tina whistled. "Now, that's the hottie I know. Want me to hold on to your dress-up clothes for you?"

"Absolutely," Jessie said. "If you can put them in the backroom I'll come get them tomorrow. Right now we've got a trip to the eighties to make."

* * *

Nick couldn't help but grin as he looked at the crowd around him. There were women with net shirts, satin gloves, and insanely teased hair. Men with acid wash jeans and neon muscle shirts. He even saw a few Mohawks.

"It's like the eighties threw up in here," he said, but Jessie didn't hear him over the din of the retro dance tunes that blasted over the loudspeakers.

She seemed to be in her element. Everyone knew her, from the bouncer at the door to the DJ in the booth. She'd been trying to lead them to a table since the moment they'd stepped inside, but people stopped her every thirty seconds to say hello or give her a hug.

Nick was just beginning to wonder if she'd even notice if he left when she turned around and smiled apologetically. She stood on tiptoe so she could reach his ear and shouted, "Forget the table. I think we'd better just go dance."

"Dance?"

"Yeah—you know. Out there—on that big flat thing with the strobe lights?"

"I don't know…"

"I do. Now, come on," she said, and proceeded to drag him by the hand out on to the dance floor.

Damn it. Ballroom dancing was one thing. But he hadn't had much time for clubbing in recent years. He was more than a little rusty.

Before he could formulate an excuse they hit the center of the dance floor and Jessie started moving to the pounding beat.

Reluctantly, he started to shuffle and sway, trying his best to look interested without actually moving much.

Jessie rolled her eyes. "Come on, now. I *know* you've got more rhythm than that. You're not even trying. Show me your moves, Casanova!"

Seeing the challenge in her eyes, he decided to go for

broke. Roughly, he pulled her close, then set his hips working in a dirty dancing move he remembered from the eighties movies his nanny had liked to watch.

Her eyes gleamed as she picked up his rhythm, her hips rolling right along with his. Seeing her grin, he decided to push it a little farther, and before long her head was thrown back as she moved with a wild abandon that made him long to rip the neon green tube off her and work her body for real.

As if sensing his mood, she wriggled in close and hooked one leg around his hips, grinding against him in a move that was only one degree removed from sex.

His brain exploded with raw need as he kept the dance going, his breathing growing rough and broken. She looked up at him and he saw what he was feeling reflected in the deep blue of her eyes.

Taking things further would definitely be a bad idea, but he was feeling too turned on to care.

"Want to get out of here?" he asked.

She pulled back and stared for a moment, as if trying to figure out what he meant by that. He pushed his hard length against her and she gasped.

"Yes," she said, "I most certainly do. But…"

"Don't think about it," he said. "Let's just—"

Suddenly a spotlight clicked into life right over their heads.

"Let's hear it for tonight's dirtiest dancers—Jessie and her new man. I've seen Jessie doing a lot of different moves, but none this hot!"

Jessie looked as shocked as he felt, but relaxed when she heard the friendly cheers from the crowd echoing around her. Laughing, she held her middle finger up to the man in the DJ booth. "Thanks a lot, Derek."

"You're welcome, sweetheart," the voice boomed. "And since no one can possibly hope to beat your moves, it's time to bring on the night's next entertainment…karaoke, eighties-style!"

With his announcement, the glittery curtains at the end of the room were pulled back to reveal a small stage, with three microphones and a karaoke screen.

"Jessie, will you do us the honor of going first?"

Jessie held out her hands in front of her as she shook her head. "No way. I'm not here to sing tonight."

"Aw, come on. Ladies and gentlemen—help me convince Jessie to give it a try!"

Soon a chant of, "Jessie! Jessie! Jessie!" filled the small club.

She looked at him, her expression a mix of embarrassment and eagerness. "Do you mind?" she asked. "It's kind of what I'm known for around here."

Feeling equal parts fascinated and disappointed by the sudden turn of events, he shook his head. "Go ahead. I can't wait to see what you do."

"Thanks," she said, and kissed him on the cheek.

Then she made her way toward the DJ's booth as the crowd roared with approval. Nick left the dance floor and headed for a table at the corner of the stage. When a cocktail waitress appeared, he asked for two beers and two doubles of whiskey. He was certainly thirsty, and he was sure Jessie would be too when she was done on stage.

Then he sat back to watch.

Jessie had left the DJ's booth and was now moving things around on the stage. A few seconds later the lights went down and Jessie was bathed in the pink glow of a single spotlight. Her head was bent, her long red locks hiding her face. When the first chords of an eighties anthem sounded she threw her hair back, a look of wanton desire on her face.

She launched into the lyrics, her smoky soprano voice and writhing dance moves giving new life to the tired words. When she got to the chorus she went down on her knees and crawled across the stage, still singing as she headed for his corner. The crowd went wild, egging her on, and then she was crawling onto Nick's lap, making love to the microphone all the while.

By the time the song ended she was straddling him, and it was all he could do not to pick her up and carry her to some dark corner where he could peel her clothes off. Finally it was over, and the spotlight left her in the dark.

"And *that's* the way we do karaoke here, folks! Anybody want to challenge the unbeatable Jessie?" the DJ called.

The crowd surged toward the stage as Jessie and Nick stared at each other. He felt paralyzed with want, with every fiber of his being begging him to kiss her. But before he could move she swooped down and claimed his lips with her own.

There was nothing soft or unsure about her kiss. It was hard, and demanding, and raw with need. He answered in kind, threading his hand through her red mane and pulling her even closer as his tongue teased her lips open. She groaned as she gave way, and soon their tongues battled for control. He plunged deeper and deeper into the warm cavern of her mouth, suddenly desperate to have as much of her as he could manage.

If only they were somewhere a little more private...

As if sensing his thoughts, she broke away, her body shaking.

"Take me home. *Now.*"

"I thought you'd never ask." Grabbing his phone, he sent a quick text to his driver, and was pleased when he got an immediate response. "We've got five minutes to get ourselves to the front door."

She didn't need to be told twice. Quickly, she slid off his lap and led him into the dark shadows on the fringes of the club.

"Let's go this way. That way no one will stop us," she said, guiding him out through a fire door.

"Won't the alarm…?"

"Don't worry. It's disabled."

He nodded, letting out a groan of relief when the cool night air hit his overheated skin. "That feels amazing."

She kissed him again. "No, *you* feel amazing. Let's go grab our taxi before someone else steals it."

"Oh, we don't have to take a taxi. I called Bob."

"Bob?"

"My driver," he said.

"Oh…" she replied, a frown wrinkling her brow.

"Is something the matter?"

"What? No. Of course not."

Jessie let Nick lead her to the limo waiting in front of the club.

"Hi, Bob," he said to the uniformed man holding the door open.

"Hi, yourself. Where are you two headed?"

Nick motioned for her to slide in. "My place."

The driver nodded. "Very well," he said, slamming the door shut before going to take his place behind the wheel.

Jessie shivered—and only partly from the cold. Now that they were out of the club and back in Nick's world she couldn't stop thinking that this—that *they*—were all wrong.

She wasn't afraid to have casual sex with someone she was attracted to, but sleeping with Nick would be a mistake.

After all, just a few hours ago he had reminded her that he wouldn't hesitate to crush her agency if he got the chance. Giving in to whatever this was between them would only make their real lives more difficult.

Leaning forward, she knocked on the glass that separated them from the driver.

He slid it open. "Yes?"

"Actually, Bob, I'd like you to take me home. Do you remember where that is?"

"Of course, miss. I couldn't forget that pink brownstone of yours if I tried."

"Thanks, Bob," she said, then turned to look at Nick.

"I can't do this."

"Oh, come on, Jessie," he said, leaning over to trail kisses on her neck. "You know you want to. Come home with me. I promise you won't regret it."

She gasped as his lips brushed the pulse-point at the base of her throat, sending a spike of desire straight into her gut. Maybe he was right. There was no reason this had to be any different than any other late-night hookup.

But then she remembered who he was.

Groaning, she pulled away.

"No. It's a bad idea. I have to go home."

He reached for her hand, frowning when she pulled it away. "Why the change of heart?"

"You're Nicholas Thornton—second in command at of one of the biggest ad agencies in the world. And I'm Jessie—owner of the digital upstart that stole a big chunk of your business. I can't sleep with you now, knowing I'll be seeing you in the boardroom in a few days. And that you'll be trying to ruin me when we're there."

Nick shook his head. "You are not Roar. I don't want to ruin *you*."

"It doesn't matter. The end result is the same."

Nick's cocky smile was back. "I know an easy way to fix the problem. Just tell Phyllis that you don't think Roar is capable of handling the launch alone."

Jessie threw her hands up in the air. "And now we're back to that. Bob, why don't you just let me out here?"

"Nonsense, miss. We'll see you home. My mother would have my hide if I let a woman like you walk home alone."

"He's right," Nick said. "There's no way you're getting out of this car. We'll take you home."

She sighed. "Fine. Have it your way."

The rest of the ride passed in awkward silence. Jessie spent the time silently listing all the reasons why having sex with Nick was a bad idea and trying not to inhale the spicy deliciousness that was his scent. Finally the limo slowed and the driver got out.

"Thank you for a wonderful evening," she said.

"You're sure you won't change your mind?"

She squeezed his hand. "I'm sure."

He lifted her hand to his mouth and kissed the sensitive skin on her inner wrist. "And *I* am sure that there will soon come a night when you will."

She laughed to cover up the hunger his kisses awoke in her. "Don't count on it."

The car door opened and Bob stood waiting.

"Too late. I already am," said Nick as she slid out into the cool night air.

Unable to think of an appropriate reply, she shook her head and fled up the steps to her house. She couldn't help but notice that the limo stayed until the door was closed firmly behind her. Nick might be dangerous, but he was still a gentleman.

"What a night," she said to herself as she kicked off her shoes and headed up the old wooden staircase to her apartment.

"Whoa, that's *not* what you were wearing when you left," her sister said when she flopped down on the couch next to her.

"No, it's definitely not. We stopped in at Tina's."

Gloria pulled a confused face. "How do you start at a charity ball and end up at Tina's Thrift Shop?"

"I wanted to take him dancing at Happy Hour."

"Okay, that makes sense. *Not*. You'd better start at the beginning."

Jessie sighed, suddenly feeling exhausted. "Not until I have a glass of wine in my hand."

"Red, white or bubbles?" her sister asked as she padded into the kitchen that opened off the living room.

"Red."

Jessie heard the reassuring gurgle of wine being poured into a glass.

"Uh-oh. That means it ended badly. I was hoping for bubbles."

"Not badly. Just realistically. Which is kind of the same thing in this case."

"Okay," Gloria said as she brought their wine glasses over. "Let's start at the beginning. Was he Prince Charming or the evil stepbrother?"

Jessie took a slow sip before answering. "Charming."

"Is he a suit or a player?"

"Neither."

"Can he dance?"

An image of his rolling hips slid through her mind. "Yes."

"Did he make you laugh?"

"Yes."

"You kissed, didn't you?"

Jessie sighed. "Oh, yes."

Gloria put her hand up for a high-five. "You're shameless—you know that?"

Jessie could feel the smirk that turned up the corners of her lips. "What? It's not like I slept with him."

Gloria took a slow sip of her wine. "What stopped you?"

"You mean apart from the fact that he runs the agency whose biggest account we just stole?"

"Yes, apart from that. A couple of years ago that wouldn't have stopped you."

Jessie shrugged. "Nick lives in a different world. He's filthy rich and he's lived his entire life around other filthy rich people. It's almost obscene, the way those people throw around money."

"Since when do you have an objection to being rich? I thought that was where we were trying to get with Roar."

"I wouldn't mind being rich. But I *do* mind being looked down upon because I'm not already."

"Was he doing that?"

"No," Jessie said, struggling to find a way to put what she was feeling into words. "Actually, he was wonderfully normal. I can't remember the last time I had that much fun with a guy. If he was someone else I would have totally gone for it."

Gloria gave her a pitying look. "I know what your problem is."

"So do I. He's the guy that wants to crush my agency. 'Like a bug,' he said."

Gloria waved her hand carelessly. "Which is why the fact that you might actually *feel* something for this guy scares you."

Jessie snorted. "Trust me. That's not the problem."

"Yes, it is. At least part of it. Somehow this one's gotten under your skin."

Jessie choked on her wine. "That's ridiculous. You know as well as I do that love just isn't in the cards for me."

"That's what you keep saying, sis," Gloria answered, rolling her eyes. "But I don't know why."

"You saw what happened to Dad. That was all the proof I ever needed that love isn't worth it. I never want to be that dependent on someone."

Gloria's eyes softened. "It doesn't always end that way."

"I know."

But it didn't matter. She'd seen the way her father had wasted away after her mother died. Nothing had mattered to him anymore—not even the two teenage daughters who'd needed him so much. It had taken him six months to have the heart attack that killed him, but he'd been as good as dead the moment they'd put his wife—their mother—in the ground.

She never wanted to know what *that* felt like.

"Listen. It's late, and this conversation has gotten altogether too deep. I'm going to head off to bed, okay?"

Gloria nodded. "Sweet dreams."

Jessie nodded back and shuffled off. But even as she put on her favorite flannel pajamas and snuggled deep under the covers she knew sleep would be a long time coming.

Her brain was determined to replay the night—and her conversation with Gloria. In her heart of hearts she was afraid Gloria was right. Nick hadn't gotten to her yet, but there was a chance that he might. And even if it wasn't for their business situation that would never do.

She'd go ahead and wallow tonight. But tomorrow it would be back to business as usual—which meant these fantasies about Nick would be left at the curb.

CHAPTER FOUR

NICK WAS JUST sitting down at his desk, coffee in hand, when his IM pinged.

Need you in my office. Now.

For a moment he was too surprised that his dad knew how to instant message to react. And when he realized that his dad was actually in the office on a Sunday his jaw practically hit the floor. This was his day to be on the golf course—"networking" over balls and beers. What on earth was he doing here?

Is this thing on?

He chuckled to himself. His father was no more patient in text than he was on the phone.

Yep. I'll be right there.

Apparently he wasn't going to have the peaceful day he had hoped for.

Sighing, he picked up his coffee cup and headed down the hall to his father's corner office. The hallways were dark, lit only by the emergency lights. That was weird in and of itself. When he'd last worked in this building it had almost always been buzzing—weekends included.

Things had either gotten a lot more laidback while he

was gone, or the company was in more trouble than his father was letting on.

Since his father's door was open, he didn't bother to knock.

"Hey, Dad," he said as he padded across the thick cream-colored carpet, temporarily blinded by the bright morning sunlight that flooded the room.

In contrast to the dark wood and heavy furniture that dominated the rest of the offices, his father had redone his office to reflect the latest trends. It was all chrome and glass and shiny surfaces.

Nick couldn't help but wonder if it was his father's attempt to look relevant.

"Are you wearing *flip-flops*? In the *office*?"

Nick shrugged. The faded T-shirt, jeans and flip-flops he was wearing were his normal weekend attire. He'd seen no reason to dress up today. He sat down in the uncomfortable metal chair in front of his father's desk and put his feet up on the glass tabletop.

"Yeah. Why? You got a client who wants to meet on a Sunday?"

His father frowned. "No. It just seems inappropriate. You're a role model here. You should dress like one."

Nick laughed. "There's no one here!"

"Still, I remember when…"

Nick groaned. "Did you call me down here to talk about the past again?"

His father's face tightened, and if Nick wasn't mistaken he saw hurt flash across his face. "No. Of course not. I wanted to talk about your proposal."

"What proposal?"

"The one we were talking about the other night. About establishing a digital agency here."

Nick sat up straighter in his chair. "Of course. What do you think, now that you've had time to consider it?"

His father leaned forward in his chair, placing his hands flat on the desk.

"I admit I wasn't wild about the idea at first. But I got to talking to some of our colleagues at the Goddess event the other night and it looks like you might be right. They were all talking about how well their digital arms were doing for them, and about how much room there is to grow in the online space. They're treating it as the way forward."

"Which is what I tried to tell you—"

"I'm not done," his father snapped. "After the ball I came back here and dug into the sales reports and board updates from London in the five years that you were there. I was impressed by what I saw."

"I thought you knew what I'd done? That's why you agreed to let me come back and fix things here, isn't it?"

"I knew you were doing well. I didn't know *why* you were doing so well. Now I do."

Nick smiled. It was about time his father acknowledged his success. "So, now that you do, are you prepared to listen to me?"

"Yes. I want you to take Thornton digital. In fact that's the name I've put on the incorporation documents I'm having drafted: Thornton Digital. You'll be president and CEO, and you'll have *carte blanche* to do what you need to do to make it profitable. If you do, I'll sell you my shares and retire. You'll have majority control of the agency and be able to veto anything the board comes up with."

Stunned, Nick sat forward, letting his feet slam to the floor. His father was giving him far more than he'd hoped for.

"There are only two conditions."

He should have known there'd be a catch. "What?"

"First you've got to get Goddess back."

Nick nodded. "Of course." He'd expected that.

"And you've got to show a profit within three months."

"You're kidding, right?" That was nowhere near enough time.

His father shook his head. "No. That's when the board is meeting to decide whether or not to sell. If we can't prove that Thornton is worth keeping by then, they'll accept the first offer they get."

Nick slumped back in his chair. "You got any alcohol in here?"

"Of course. Whiskey or Scotch?"

"Whiskey."

His father nodded and walked over to the bar discreetly tucked into a corner. As he prepared their drinks Nick thought furiously. How the hell was he going to pull this off? It was an impossible task.

Or was it?

By the time his father handed him his drink he had a plan.

"Question for you, Dad."

"Hold on. Something tells me I'm going to want to be sitting down for this." Before saying anymore he pulled out his chair, propped his feet up, and took a deep drink. "All right—shoot."

Nick took a deep breath. "When you said I had *carte blanche*, did you really mean it?"

"Yes…why?"

"I want to buy Roar."

His father sputtered, nearly choking on his drink. "You want to *what*?"

"Buy out Roar. Jessie already has a talented group of employees, a big chunk of business that we want, and a feminist world view that's entirely missing from this company. With her on our side we could easily hit the numbers we need before the board meets."

His father was silent for a long moment as he sipped his drink. Finally he nodded.

"Hmm. I like where you're going with this. Two birds… one stone. Do you think she'll bite?"

Nick grinned. "I'm sure I can convince her. I'll make her a vice president—maybe put her in charge of the creative side…and throw a wad of cash at her. It'll be a great opportunity for both sides."

"You seem very confident that you can win her over. Why *is* that? I saw you leaving the gala with her. Are you romantically involved?"

"No, of course not. She wasn't feeling well, so I took her home." That was almost the truth—the evening certainly hadn't ended on a romantic note.

"Good. Now that you're taking on a leadership role here people are going to expect you to take your place in society. You need a proper wife, who knows how to entertain and conduct herself in public. Not some wild party girl."

"Dad. You know I'm never getting married. I don't care what society thinks." Nick sighed, running his hands through his hair. "But I don't want to talk about it right now. Can we get back to the subject at hand? If you're amenable to the idea, I need to get a proposal together."

His father stood. "All right. What do we have to lose? Put some numbers together as fast as you can. I'm going to have my secretary set a meeting for Tuesday afternoon."

Nick nodded and left, already busy crunching numbers in his head. He knew joining forces would work out amazingly well for both sides. Together, they'd be unbeatable in the boardroom. And once they were no longer competing against each other it would be far simpler to convince her to start sleeping together too.

Jessie took a deep breath and squared her shoulders before exiting through the car door Nick's driver held open for her.

"Thanks, Bob," she said.

"No problem, miss. Just doing my job. Knock 'em dead in there."

"I'll try!"

The big man looked at her with a reassuring smile. "Don't let him intimidate you. Brad farts and burps just like everyone else."

Jessie smiled. "I'll remember that." Then she set off for the big glass doors, ready to face the dragon.

She'd been shocked when Brad's assistant had called yesterday to schedule a meeting. She'd gotten the impression from Nick that he was pretty hands-off—all the more so since Goddess was an account that Nick managed.

She couldn't help but wonder why *she* rated a personal meet-and-greet with the great man himself, never mind the door-to-door car service he'd insisted must go along with it.

No sooner had she stepped into the lobby than a tall, thin blond intercepted her. "You must be Jessie," she said.

"Um, yes, I am. I'm here for a meeting with Mr. Thornton."

"Oh, yes, I know," the woman said. "I'm here to give you a personal tour of our space before the meeting."

"Oh," Jessie said, feeling more confused than ever. "And you are…?"

"Ingrid. I'm one of the assistant creative directors here. Brad thought you might appreciate a woman's perspective on our company."

"Why?" Jessie asked, alarm bells going off in her brain. "I'm not interviewing for a job or anything."

Just then Nick appeared, his five o'clock shadow making him look even more ruggedly handsome than usual.

"Jessie, I'm so glad you came," he said, reaching out to shake her hand. "My father and I were worried that you might have gotten the wrong impression about us—seeing how we got off on the wrong foot and all. We wanted to give you another perspective on our work before you hear our proposal."

Jessie snatched her hand back, doing her best to ignore the tingles his touch had set off in her arms. "What proposal?"

Nick beamed at her. "I can't tell you yet. But I think you're going to love it."

"Nick—" Jessie started, but he didn't give her a chance to finish.

"I've got to run a quick errand, so I'll leave you in Ingrid's capable hands. See you in a few minutes!"

And with that he set off again, his quick strides taking him out into the sunshine in a matter of seconds. Jessie sighed, then turned to the supermodel beside her. She had no idea what was going on, but for now it seemed best to play along.

"All right, Ingrid. Why don't you show me what Thornton is all about?"

As Ingrid chattered on about flexible hours and job-sharing Jessie tuned out, looking at her surroundings instead. Everything from the marble lobby to the maze of cubicles on the floors above reminded her of her years in corporate agency life. She didn't miss anything about it. Especially not the politics. And now, thanks to the trust Goddess was putting in them, she was confident that she'd never have to go back. Thank goodness.

She'd never forgotten her mother's last words to her. "Life is shorter than you think. Try to spend every minute of it doing something you love," she'd said. And Jessie had done her best.

After Becky, her best friend and creative partner, had left the agency where they'd worked all the fun had gone out of it. That was when she'd known it was time to step out of the corporate box and go to work for herself.

"Do you have any questions?" Ingrid asked, and Jessie realized they were standing outside a conference room.

Since she hadn't heard a single word the woman had said, she definitely didn't. She just shook her head and smiled.

"Thank you for the tour, Ingrid. I really appreciate it." Then she was struck by a thought. Maybe this agency was more enlightened than the ones she'd worked for. "Hey, I do have one question. How many women are in management here?"

Ingrid looked taken aback. "Oh. Er, there's just me," she said. "Although many of our senior creatives are women!"

Same story—different agency. "Okay, cool. I was just curious. Thanks again!"

The other woman smiled and disappeared into the maze of cubicles, leaving Jessie alone in the hallway.

"Guess it's time to learn about this fabulous proposal," she said to herself. Then, pulling herself to her full height, she entered the conference room.

She'd been expecting a typical cavernous corporate boardroom, so the cozy set-up of overstuffed couches and chairs facing each other around an oversized coffee table threw her for a loop. The only sign that it was a conference room at all was the floor-to-ceiling projector screen that was set up on one wall.

Brad was at an antique-looking sideboard, fussing with a mug of coffee.

"Jessie!" he said. "Thank you for coming. Would you like some coffee?"

"Oh," she said, surprised to see him pouring for himself. "Sure—that would be great."

A moment later he brought her a gleaming green and gold mug. "Sit wherever you like. We'll get started just as soon as Nick arrives."

"Is it just the three of us?" she asked, weighing her seating options.

Sitting on a sofa just seemed weird—plus she didn't really want Brad to think he could sit next to her—so she chose a brown leather armchair and carefully set her cup on the glass top of the coffee table.

"Yes. We thought it would be best to keep this discussion quiet for now. Tell me, do you enjoy running your agency...Roar, isn't it?"

"I do. This past year has been difficult, but all the hard work is starting to pay off now."

"Indeed it is—much to our chagrin," the older man said, a rueful smile on his face. "I certainly admire your entrepreneurial spirit."

"Thank you. What about you? Was running an advertising agency always your dream?"

He set his mug down with a clang, clearly surprised by her question. "I never had to dream about it. Thornton simply *was*, and it was my duty to take the reins when my father passed on."

"My father is big on duty," Nick said as he pushed into the room. "And I'm all about passion. It makes for interesting meetings."

"Nick, it's about time you joined us. He's right, but there's one other ingredient in our recipe for success that he forgot to mention. Innovation."

"Innovation?" she repeated, trying to ignore the way her pulse jumped when Nick brushed by her on his way to a seat.

"That's right. And our latest innovation is right up your alley. Nick, why don't you tell her about it?"

Nick looked at his father, his eyes pinched with annoyance. "Well, I *had* hoped to set the stage a little more, but all right—let's get down to business. As I said before, we have a proposal for you that I think you're really going to like."

Jessie took a deep breath, trying to ignore the voice at the back of her mind yelling *Get out before it's too late!*

"Okay. I'm listening."

Nick gave her a reassuring smile. "Jessie, what you've accomplished with Roar in such a short time is nothing less than amazing. You're making digital work for your clients in ways that I didn't even know were possible."

As he piled on the praise Jessie's hackles rose. What on earth was his game? This current line of thinking didn't seem to go along with his earlier "I'll crush you like a bug" statements.

His next words made her snap back to attention. "Jessie, there's no one I'd rather have by my side as I start my next venture—Thornton Digital."

Jessie felt her jaw drop open. "What?"

"I'd like you to be my second in command," Nick said, excitement plain in the grin on his face. "My woman in the trenches. I'll be in charge of finances and big picture stuff—you can handle the creative side. Together, I know we can run circles around the competition."

"But I already *have* an agency. *I* run it. *All* of it. Why would I leave that behind?"

He leaned forward and touched her hand. "Actually, we'd like to buy Roar from you and make your people the foundation of Thornton Digital."

Jessie snatched her hand back. "You want to buy Roar?" she said, not letting herself show any emotion.

"Yes." His expression was serious now.

"And you want my people to come work for you?"

He shook his head. "No, I want your people to continue to work for *you*. As Thornton Digital employees."

Jessie stared at him for a moment, still trying to figure out what his game was. Why would he suddenly want to join forces? There had to be a trick. But he appeared sincere—no agency-eating shark in sight.

"Uh-huh. And why would I want to sell to you, exactly?"

"We're prepared to make you quite a generous offer," Brad broke in, sliding a manila folder in front of her.

She opened the folder with a shaking hand, expecting to see a detailed contract. Instead, there was just a check—a check with more zeroes on it than she'd ever seen in her life.

"Wow…" she breathed, unable to keep the word from sliding out of her mouth.

"As my son said, we realize how much potential Roar has. We arrived at this number after calculating a conservative estimate of what your profits might be over the next ten years. This would allow you to pay off the business loan, the mortgage you had to put on your house, and to live very comfortably even if you never work another day in your life."

Her mind was reeling. Weren't loans supposed to be private transactions? "How do you know about those?"

"There's very little I can't find out if I set my mind to it," the elder Thornton said. "This isn't all we're prepared to offer, either. As Executive Vice President of Thornton Digital, you'll have an annual salary of two hundred and fifty thousand dollars, with profit-sharing and annual bonuses."

Jessie blinked. *Hard.* Although what they were offering was a life-changing amount of money, her stomach churned at the idea of giving up her freedom and going corporate again. But would her sister feel the same way?

Jessie knew she owed it to Gloria at least to run the idea by her. But what if she wanted to accept it? She couldn't take that chance. If worst came to worst she could always buy Gloria out—she only had a ten percent stake in the business.

She took a deep breath, then looked up at Nick. His expression was guarded, his earlier enthusiasm banked. Jessie had a strange feeling that he knew what she was going to say.

"Thank you, gentlemen. This is a very generous offer,

and I am honored to know that you think so highly of me and my business. But I'm afraid I can't take it. Roar is not for sale and neither am I."

Nick frowned. "I know this would be a big change for you, but I think you owe it to yourself to give it some thought. This could take your career to a whole new level—and give you access to clients you could never get on your own."

She raised an eyebrow. "Clients like Goddess, you mean? Because I didn't need any help from a corporate big brother to land that one."

"No, you didn't. But you can't hope to continue to have that kind of success. Roar's not big enough to compete on that level."

"Why not?"

Nick let loose a short bark of laughter, an incredulous look on his face. "Oh, come *on*, now. You run Roar out of your *house*! You must know that if Phyllis saw your set-up she'd realize that your agency doesn't belong in the big league. It all looks very amateurish."

Jessie gasped, feeling as if she'd been slapped. "Is that what you think I am?" she asked, hating the quaver that had found its way into her voice. "An amateur? And here I thought you were actually beginning to respect me."

Nick frowned again. "Of course I respect you. We wouldn't offer to hire you if we didn't. But Roar…? It's not going to take you where you want to go."

Anger flared to life, and it was hard to get the next words out through the roaring in her skull. "Nothing about Roar is amateur. We're on to something big and you know it. And, unfortunately for you, we're not about to let a bunch of testosterone-addled bigwigs screw it up—no matter how much you throw at us."

"Jessie—" Nick started, anger flashing in his eyes.

"No, let me finish. Roar is taking me *exactly* where I

want to go—on my terms. I don't want to go anywhere on yours."

Nick glared at her. "Are you finished now?"

"Yes," she said, lifting her chin defiantly.

Nick took a deep breath. "Jessie, I am going to chalk your immediate reaction—and your words—up to shock. Please take a few days to think about our proposal. I believe you'll find it's in your best interests to accept."

"I'll pretend to think about it, if you want. But I'm not going to change my mind."

"Then Roar is finished," Brad said, his expression dangerously calm. "We'll do whatever it takes to make sure you never get another scrap of business."

Jessie's blood boiled. "Go ahead and try. I'd rather live out of my car than work for the likes of *you*."

Picking up her briefcase, she stomped out of the conference room.

Nick opened the door to go after Jessie. "Great parting words, Dad," Nick said over his shoulder. "I'm sure she'll seriously consider our proposal now."

"Forget about her. One way or the other, we're getting rid of Roar."

Nick shook his head as he strode out of the conference room. He saw her standing red-faced at the elevator bank, angrily punching the "down" arrow.

"Jessie! Wait!" he shouted.

Mutely, she shook her head and continued stabbing the button, looking surprised when a set of doors opened in front of her. Nick sprinted down the hall and skidded inside the elevator before it could close.

"What do you want?" she asked, her blue eyes sparking fire as the doors closed behind him.

"I wanted to apologize for the amateur comment. It came out wrong. I respect what you're doing and I hope you'll at least consider our proposal. You and I—we could be great together."

"And if I don't sign on the dotted line?"

Nick shrugged. "Then I'll enjoy beating you every time we compete against each other for a client."

Jessie's lips twisted. "Unless you destroy us first?"

Nick winced. "Listen, I'm sorry about what my father said. He doesn't always handle things in the most diplomatic way possible."

"Oh, I think he handled it exactly right. Now your offer doesn't look even the faintest bit tempting—no matter how many zeroes are on it."

"I'm sorry to hear that," he said, mentally stomping on the impulse to run his hands through that wild red hair.

She must have seen the heat in his eyes, because she flushed and looked away.

"Listen, just stay away. Stay away from me. Stay away from Roar. We don't need anything from the Thorntons."

The elevator dinged with impeccable timing, and before he could say another word she was walking away.

"You might not need anything from the Thorntons," he said to himself as he pushed the "up" button, "but this Thornton sure wants something from you."

Actually, he wanted all of her. Naked. Spread out on his bed.

He only hoped he could bury this irrational need for Jessie's touch in work.

CHAPTER FIVE

"THEY OFFERED YOU *what*, now?" Gloria said, her cereal spoon dangling limply from her hand.

"Fifty million dollars," Jessie answered between bites of yogurt.

"And you turned them down?"

"Yes, of course," Jessie said. "Wouldn't you have?"

"Look, I love Roar as much as you do—at least I thought I did—but I would have jumped on that buyout offer."

"Why?"

"That much money would give you the financial freedom to do anything you want. You could start a new agency. Start a cancer foundation. Buy an island in the South Pacific! *Anything!*"

"Yes, but I'd be giving up on Roar. On my hope of proving to the world that women-run agencies can compete with the big guys."

Gloria slumped back against her chair, her brunette hair catching the morning sunlight as she ran frustrated hands through it.

"I guess that's where we're different," she said.

"How?"

"I see this as a job. A cool job—but a job. You see it as a mission."

Jessie shrugged. "I guess I do. But, listen, if you want out I'll buy your share."

"No, that's not what I want. It's just… I wish…" Gloria's mouth snapped closed.

"You wish what?"

"Nothing." Gloria got up and carried her dishes over to the sink. "Will you do me a favor?" she asked as she put them in the dishwasher.

"Sure—what?"

"Well, you're the one that's always reminding me that Mom wanted us to suck every drop of joy out of life that we could. Do you think she would have wanted you to spend your best years chained to your desk? Or would she have told you to take this money and see where your dreams can take you?"

Jessie put her head in her hands. "But I *do* love Roar. It *does* bring me joy," she said, trying to sort through the barrage of emotions assaulting her senses.

Gloria put a hand on her back.

"I know. But what about a husband? Or a family? Don't you think those things would be worth having too?"

"What? *No*," she said, sitting up so she could look at her sister. "I thought we agreed that those things were not for us? Too much chance of it all going wrong. Of ending up broken-hearted and unable to care for the other people who love you."

"I used to think that. But now I don't know. I'm tired of being alone. And, as much as I like coming home to you, I'd rather have a big strong house-husband meet me at the door, with a glass of wine in one hand and a bar of chocolate in the other."

Jessie giggled at the image. "*Sheesh*. Turn my entire world upside down, why don't you? But, as nice as that sounds, I don't think it's for me."

"Not even if the house-husband in question was a certain advertising executive named Nick?"

"*Especially* not if he was Nick," Jessie said.

But there was a twinge in her heart. A twinge that said she might be lying to herself a little. A twinge that shouldn't be there.

Suddenly angry, Jessie got up from the table and stomped down the front stairs.

Work would straighten her out. It always did.

Unfortunately more bad news was waiting in her inbox. The custom-made computers she had ordered were on back order again, and wouldn't be arriving for another three weeks. The new web developer she'd hired had emailed saying he'd gotten a better offer elsewhere, so would be unable to begin work the next Monday. And one of her hot new business prospects—an online clothing designer that she'd thought was as good as hers—had canceled their appointment that afternoon.

"What the hell?" Jessie yelled out loud. "Is the universe out to get me or something?"

Only silence answered her. Every one of her staff of twelve had noise-canceling headphones glued to their heads and were so deep in their work they had no idea she was even there.

"Great," she muttered. "Now I'm talking to myself. Time to go for a walk."

The early spring weather had taken a turn for the worse, so Jessie piled on her lavender ski jacket and headed out.

As she walked she remembered Brad Thornton's parting shot. He'd all but promised to sabotage her business. Were today's troubles part of his vendetta against her? She wouldn't have thought he could move that fast, but who knew?

Realizing she didn't have enough proof to make a case, she decided to shelve the thought for the time being and get back to work. Hopefully the afternoon would go better.

Unfortunately her hopes were dashed the moment she walked in the door.

"Um, Jessie?" Gloria said.

"Yeah?" Jessie replied as she shrugged off her coat.

"Did you know Coleen was quitting?"

"No. Wait. *What?*"

"She just told me while you were out. Today's her last day."

"You're kidding me," Jessie said. She was the lead designer on the Goddess account. No *way* could she leave!

"I wish I was."

"But she can't leave today—what about her two weeks' notice?"

"Two weeks is customary, but it's not a statutory requirement—you know that."

"We'll just have to see about that," she muttered.

Without another word, she stomped off to Coleen's desk and tugged the headphones off her ears.

"Hey!" she protested.

"Don't you *hey* me. Gloria told me you said you're quitting?"

"She's right."

Jessie felt the first stirrings of panic flutter in her stomach. "But you can't quit! We need you! The Goddess launch is less than six weeks away!"

Coleen sighed and scrubbed her hands through her hair. "I know, and I feel awful, but I've had an offer I can't refuse."

"What happened? Did someone back a truckload of cash up to your door or something?"

Coleen squirmed in her seat. "Kind of. Thornton & Co. offered to triple my salary—and give me six weeks of vacation. But to get it I have to leave you now. With no notice. I'm so sorry!"

Jessie sighed. She knew there was no way Coleen could turn down that kind of money. She was a single mom with two kids at home. She needed every penny she could get.

"*Damn*, girl. I'd try to make a counter-offer, but there's

no way I can beat that. I don't suppose you'd accept cup-cakes in lieu of cash?"

Coleen squeezed her hand. "I'm sorry, Jessie. But I have to take it."

Jessie quashed her anger and gave Coleen a sad smile. "I understand. However, I *am* going to need you to sign a nondisclosure agreement. I don't want anything we've done here to show up in one of their ads."

"I would never do that," Coleen protested.

"Right. And if I had asked you yesterday you would have said you wouldn't leave me without notice, either. I'd like it in writing, if it's all the same to you."

Coleen's shoulders slumped as she nodded. "Point taken. Okay, I'll sign whatever you need me to sign. I certainly don't want to ruin what we've started."

"Thank you. I appreciate it. I'll call our lawyer and we'll have something for you to put your X on by the end of the day."

When the woman nodded, Jessie turned to go back to her office. She'd made it no more than two steps before she saw another hand waving at her timidly from the back of the room. Every clack of her stilettos sounded like another nail in Roar's coffin as she made her way back to her lead copywriter's desk.

"What's up, Sharon?" she asked, trying to pump a cheer-fulness she didn't feel into her words.

"Um, well…" the slight woman started.

Jessie heaved a sigh. "Let me guess. Thornton Digital has made you an offer you can't refuse?"

Sharon gazed up at her with awe on her face. "How did you know?"

"I just spoke to your partner."

"Delilah? Why would she have…?"

Jessie shook her head. "No. Your work partner."

"Oh. Right. Coleen…"

"The one and only. So let me guess. Today is your last day?"

"It has to be," Sharon said sadly.

Jessie took a deep breath, trying to stay calm, despite the panic beating in her brain. "All right. But you know I have to make you sign a nondisclosure, right?"

Sharon nodded. "Whatever you need. I do feel bad about this, but with this raise we can finally afford to have a baby."

Jessie clasped her shoulder. "Don't worry. I understand. I just wish I could offer as much as they can."

"Well, when you can I'll come running back," Sharon said.

"I'll hold you to that," Jessie replied.

Once back in her office, she gave in to the anger scorching through her veins. Now that she had proof about who was behind her troubles it was time to call him on it.

She punched Nick's number into her desk phone and waited impatiently while it rang. He'd better pick up. If he didn't she'd just march down there and confront him in person. Maybe she should take something to throw at him. Maybe…

"Hello?"

"Oh. Hello," she said, surprised out of her mental tirade.

"Who is this?"

"This is Jessica Owens, owner of Roar and soon to be your worst nightmare." Okay, that might have been a bit heavy-handed, but he'd get the picture.

"Jessie? What are you talking about?"

To his credit, he sounded genuinely confused.

"What am I talking about? I'm talking about the two employees you're stealing from me. The client you persuaded not to deal with me. And the computer equipment you arranged to be delayed."

"Whoa, whoa, whoa. Slow down. I haven't done any of those things. I've spent the entire morning looking for office space for Thornton Digital."

"Why should I believe you?"

"I think you know I'm not that evil."

"I don't know anything about you," she said, unable to keep the bitterness from her voice.

His voice gentled. "Listen, let me dig around and see what I can find out. We'll get to the bottom of this."

That was more than she had expected. "Thank you," she said.

"No problem. I'll get in touch when I know more."

After she'd hung up the phone Jessie stared into space. She wanted to believe Nick. She wanted to believe that he was different—an ad man with a soul, unlike his father. But she couldn't help but remember the way he acted whenever they were in a meeting. That man was perfectly capable of doing these things.

She sighed. Oh, well, there was nothing she could do about it right now. And, since it looked as if she was about to lose her lead creative team, she'd be better off digging into the Goddess work and figuring out what she was going to do than moping about.

It was a good thing she was an art director at heart—and a good one. If she wanted to keep this account, she was going to have to roll up her sleeves and get to work.

Nick burst into his father's office without bothering to knock.

"I hear you've been busy this morning," he said as he crossed the office and sat down in one of the black leather visitors' chairs in front of the glass and chrome desk. "What do you think you're doing?"

His dad put down the newspaper he'd been reading and

looked at Nick over the top of his glasses. "I don't know what you're talking about."

"Oh, really? So you didn't threaten Jessie's clients? Or steal two of her best people?"

"Oh. That. I was just trying to help you get Thornton Digital off to a good start."

"How does that help me?"

"Well, if you're going to start a digital agency you're going to need employees. And we know Jessie has good people—otherwise she wouldn't have managed to get as far as she has. So why not steal them? Two birds—one stone."

"It didn't occur to you that I might want to hire my own employees?"

"Well, you're going to need far more than two employees. You can hire all the rest of them! And I don't care what you do with these. You can fire them tomorrow if you want to. I just didn't want Jessie to have them."

"There are other ways to get the Goddess work back. You don't have to destroy Roar."

"It's not about the work. It's about the insult," his father said. "How did you hear about this, anyway? Have you been talking to that woman?"

"She called me, yes."

"I don't want you talking to her."

"I'm not seventeen anymore. You can't tell me what to do or who to see."

"Maybe not. But I'm still in control of the agency. Stay away from that woman or else I'll set up a meeting with the board and get the agency sold tomorrow!"

"You wouldn't dare."

"Try me."

"Wow. You really are an ass," Nick said. He was having a hard time believing this was the same man who'd used to be so passionate about the agency.

He just shrugged his shoulders. "Only if provoked. Don't do it."

Unable to think of anything to say that wouldn't sound like a teenager's tantrum, Nick got up and walked out. He started for his office, but realized he was too angry to work so headed for the elevator instead.

Damn his father anyway. If it wasn't for that man's total inability to compete in the modern world he'd already have a successful digital division at Thornton and they wouldn't be in this situation in the first place.

Instead, he was trying to save the entire agency from that dinosaur by winning a key piece of business back from a particularly smoking hottie—and now he had to add keeping his father from destroying said hottie's agency until he could convince her to sell it to his list.

He had no problem beating her in the boardroom. But these underhand tricks…? That was just bad business.

Speaking of which… He whipped out his phone and fired off a text.

Got the answers you need. Need to meet to talk.

Seconds later, her response pinged.

Okay. How about The Pub?

He started to text back that the advertising community's most popular hangout would be fine, but then realized that it would be a terrible idea. All it would take would be for one of his father's cronies to see him with her and his grandfather's legacy would disappear.

Not there. Somewhere less…popular.

Ever heard of Rachel's Diner?

No.

Great. Meet me there in an hour.

Nick stepped inside the brightly lit restaurant and grinned. It looked like Hollywood's idea of a greasy spoon, complete with chrome counters and ripped vinyl seating in the Formica-topped booths. Jessie was right. There was no chance they'd see any of his cool cat colleagues here.

"Hey, good-looking," said a large woman with caramel-colored skin who must be Rachel. "You can sit wherever you want, but I sure hope you find yourself a seat over here in my area." She waved at the entire left side of the restaurant.

"Actually, I'm looking for someone. She…"

"Oh, are you Jessie's boy? She's back in the corner over there, honey."

He looked where she pointed and saw Jessie's unmistakable red curls beckoning to him from the far corner of the restaurant. His heart skipped a beat at the sight.

"Thanks," he said, and crossed to where she was sitting. She was curled around her phone, texting furiously, and didn't see him slide into the booth.

"Are you telling all your friends about your hot date?"

She looked up, startled, relaxing only slightly when she saw it was him.

"No, just telling my lawyer about your father's hugely inappropriate antics."

Nick's heart stopped. "Seriously?"

"No. Just talking to Becky."

"Oh. Good," he said, forcing out a laugh.

An uncomfortable silence fell over the table. He knew what he had to tell Jessie, but he was so embarrassed he didn't know quite how to start. Thankfully, Rachel chose that moment to arrive.

"Jessie, when you told me you were expecting someone you should have been more descriptive. I just about had a heart attack when I saw him come through the door."

Jessie grinned. "Sorry, Rachel. I'm used to looking at him. I forget the effect he has on unsuspecting women."

Nick found himself feeling strangely flattered. It was good to know that Jessie found him just as attractive as he found her.

"So, what will you two lovebirds be having this evening?" Rachel asked.

"Burger. Fries. Chocolate shake," Jessie rattled off.

"I'll have what she's having. She's the expert."

"Coming right up," Rachel said as she hurried away.

Once she was gone, Jessie pinned him with her piercing blue eyes. "So. What did you find out?"

"You were right," he said.

"Right about what?"

"About my father. He's trying to close you down."

"Why?"

"You took a big chunk of business from him and refused to sell him your agency."

"Well, yes. But that was business. This feels personal."

"It is. You did both things while being a woman. That is an unforgivable sin in his eyes."

Jessie slumped back in the booth. "Did you tell him to back off?"

"Yes, but he didn't listen. He hardly ever does. He might have dragged me back from London to save the company, but that doesn't mean he actually trusts my advice."

"But he is obviously establishing a digital arm for the agency. That was your recommendation, I'm guessing?"

"Yes, he is." Nick said, unable to help the satisfied smile that crept on to his face. "And, supposedly, I have *carte blanche* to do whatever needs to be done to get it up and going."

"As long as 'whatever it takes' includes sending me and my employees to the unemployment line, right?"

"That seems to be his strategy, but it's not mine. Although my offer to buy Roar stands. We'd be good together—and we'd all make boatloads of cash." If only he could make her see how much sense it made for them to join forces, he wouldn't have to steal Goddess back from her.

Jessie toyed with her napkin, shredding it into little pieces. "That's good to know. But my answer is still no. I like being independent."

He decided to bait her a little. "All right—fine. I'll hire my own group of awesome women, become known as a feminist agency, and start creating kick-ass work."

Her head snapped up. "I thought you just said you weren't going to try to put me out of business?"

Nick laughed. "I'm not going to do that. I was just trying to get your goat."

"Oh." Jessie's shoulders relaxed. "Good."

Rachel arrived, carrying a loaded tray. "All right you lovebirds, it's time to dig in."

"You are a woman with impeccable timing," Nick said. "Thank you!"

"Anytime, honey."

After she'd left they busied themselves with napkins and silverware and dug in.

Nick took a bite of his hamburger and groaned out loud. "This. Is. Delicious."

Jessie nodded. "Rachel's is the best. Reminds me of this place I used to go with my mom, growing up."

"In New York?"

Jessie shook her head. "Nope. In Detroit. It was this greasy little diner down the street from our house. We'd go there every time she decided we needed some girl-time. She'd order us burgers and chocolate malts, and we wouldn't leave until we'd sorted through whatever problem I was having."

"That sounds pretty great," Nick said. He was surprised to realize he was a little jealous. His mother had certainly never spent that kind of time with *him*.

Jessie's smile turned sad. "It was. Many a childhood heartache was solved in that diner. I should ask Becky if it's still there."

"I take it you don't go there anymore?"

"Nope. Haven't been back since the day my mom took me there to tell me about her cancer." Jessie's blue eyes darkened with pain. "That pretty much ruined it."

Nick reached over to squeeze her hand. "I'm sorry."

"Don't be." She returned his squeeze and then let go, reaching for her milkshake, now half gone. "Now I have Rachel's. Totally makes up for it."

He raised his glass. "I propose a toast. To Rachel's."

She clinked it with hers. "I'll drink to that."

They spent the next two hours talking about everything and nothing. The longer they talked, the more Nick found himself attracted to Jessie. She was such a mass of contradictions. One minute she seemed like an impulsive party girl. The next she was all business. And the minute after that she segued into creative genius mode.

It didn't hurt that when she was seriously into something her eyes sparkled and her skin flushed. She looked delicious. The caveman in him wanted nothing more than to pick her up, lay her down on top of the table, and melt her into a puddle of screaming orgasm.

"What are you thinking?" she asked.

Nick blinked. What could he say that didn't sound incriminating?

"I was just thinking about how amazing you are. If things were different I'd be doing my best to sweep you off your feet right now."

She blushed, then got an evil glint in her eye. "That's very sweet of you. I wouldn't bother with sweeping you off your feet. I'd go directly to getting your clothes off."

Nick laughed. "Like I said. You're amazing. I've never met a woman like you."

Rachel bustled over. "You two need to get a move on. Chef's getting antsy. I heard him talking about bringing out the frying pan."

Nick looked around, startled. Sure enough, they were the only people left in the restaurant.

"Oh, he's all talk," Jessie said. "If I went back there he'd try and feed me a piece of pie."

Rachel smiled. "You ask me, I think he's jealous of Mr. Model over here. You've never brought us a piece of man meat before."

"Tell him not to worry," Jessie said. "We're just business associates."

Rachel stepped back, carefully evaluating them.

"Okay…sure. Just don't forget to invite me to the wedding, okay?"

Jessie rolled her eyes. "Fine, fine, whatever you say. Can we have our check now?"

"Oh! It got dark out here," Jessie said.

Time seemed to flow differently when Nick was around. When she'd left the office earlier that evening she'd had every intention of getting the information she needed from him and getting out as quickly as possible. She'd even told Gloria to text her at the half-hour mark so she could make up an excuse to go. But when the message had come she'd decided to ignore it.

She might have been eating with the enemy, but it had turned out to be the most enjoyable meal she'd eaten in quite a while.

Jessie turned to face Nick as he came out into the cold and her heart skipped a beat. He looked so solid and warm it was all she could do not to burrow under his coat. *Down girl,* she told herself. *This man is off-limits.*

"Thanks for the information," she said, wrapping her arms tightly around herself so she wouldn't give in to the impulse to snuggle up against his broad chest.

"Sure. It's the least I could do."

"I don't have any idea what I'm going to do now, though." She didn't even know where to start.

Nick waved his hand dismissively. "Don't worry about it. I'll talk my father around. He might be pig-headed, but he's not an idiot."

"I'm not sure I believe you, but I'm too worn out to care right now. I'm going to head home, okay?"

Nick nodded. "Do you want to share a cab?"

"Me? Oh, no. No, thanks. I'll just walk. It's not far." Spending any amount of time sitting next to Nick in the dark seemed like a bad idea. She wasn't sure she'd be able to keep her hands to herself.

Nick frowned. "Too far to walk alone in the dark."

"Don't worry about me. I'm tough." And she was pretty sure there was nothing in the streets as dangerous to her wellbeing as this man.

"Tough, but tiny. Let me walk you home."

"You don't have to do that," she insisted.

If he walked her home she'd have to invite him in. And if he came in—well, her bedroom was far too close for comfort.

"Nope, I don't. But I want to," he said, holding out his hand.

Obviously he wasn't going to take no for an answer.

"Fine," she said, slipping her glove-clad hand into his bare one. "But don't complain to me when your hands fall off from frostbite."

He snorted. "It's not *that* cold. Besides, having you this close to me makes me feel plenty warm."

Jessie knew what he meant. His touch sent invisible sparks traveling up her fingers and through her arm, dancing dangerously close to her heart before heading to regions farther south.

"What was the sigh about?" he asked, bringing her out of her reverie.

"Oh, nothing. Just wishing it was spring."

"I know what you mean," he said as they started their stroll. "Spring has always been my favorite season in New York. I remember one year in high school I went walking through Central Park every afternoon in April, picking all the daffodils I saw for my girlfriend."

"That's so sweet! Why did you do that?"

"They were her favorite. And she said if I brought her every daffodil in Central Park she'd have sex with me."

"And did she?"

Nick's smile turned sad. "She did. On a blanket under a tree in a quiet corner of Central Park, as a matter of fact."

Try though she might, Jessie couldn't help but imagine what that would be like. "That sounds romantic."

"Well, I was a pretty clumsy lover at that point, so I was hoping the setting would distract her."

"Did she come back for more?"

Nick smiled down at her. "Did she ever. We went at it like a couple of rabbits that spring."

Jessie grinned. "Then I'm guessing you did just fine?"

"Yeah. It was one of those fabulous teen love affairs you read about in books. We thought we'd be together forever."

He looked so sad Jessie's heart broke a little. "What happened?"

"My dad thought we were getting too serious. So he paid her to go away."

Jessie stopped dead in the middle of the sidewalk. "*Really?* Your dad offered your girlfriend money to break up with you? And she did?"

Nick nodded, obviously trying as hard as he could to look nonchalant. "Really."

"Wow. I don't know which one of them is worse. Your father for offering, or her for selling out."

Nick shrugged. "They're both pretty terrible human beings."

"Damn. I didn't think people like that really existed."

"New York is full of them, sweetheart," he said, his voice tight with bitterness.

"Not *my* New York," she said, looking at the faceless crowd swirling around them on the sidewalk. "My New York is full of weirdoes and drama queens and misunderstood geniuses. But not people like that."

"I think I like your New York better," he said, looking at her with eyes full of sadness and desire.

They drew her in like a magnet, and before she could stop herself she reached up on her tiptoes. "I think I like you," she whispered as she touched her lips to his.

When their lips connected, her world shrank until all she was aware of was the exquisite sensation of his mouth on hers. The kiss started soft and tender, speaking of shared losses and unspoken regrets. Then he groaned and wrapped his arms around her, almost crushing her against his solid warmth as his tongue sought entrance to her mouth.

She gave way as something deeper than desire flooded her body, demanding that she get closer to him. Her hands found their way around his neck and she twined herself around him as his tongue flicked around hers, hard and fast, plunging into her mouth over and over again. Heat flared deep in her belly and she whimpered involuntarily, wanting more.

"Get a room!" a rough voice shouted.

The moment was broken. The city once again filled her consciousness and she broke away, panting. *Wow. That wasn't supposed to happen.*

"Sorry." She tilted her head down so he wouldn't see how much their kiss had affected her. "I didn't mean to jump you in public."

"Don't be sorry. That was amazing," he said, his voice husky with need. "In fact, I think we should take that man's suggestion. There must be a hotel around here somewhere."

She laughed. "What happened to sweeping me off my feet?"

"I'll sweep you off your feet…on to a bed."

Now that their kiss was over her brain was back online, reminding her again of what a bad idea that would be.

Looking around, she realized they were standing on her street corner. "Sorry, Casanova. Not tonight."

Nick kissed the hand he still held. "You sure? I'll make it worth your while."

Jessie shivered. Every fiber of her being wanted to go with him. "I'm sure. In fact, my place is right down the street. We should probably say goodnight right here."

"Nah, I'll go with you. I'm not done trying to convince you to see things my way."

She wasn't sure what to say to that, so she nodded and set off down the block. They walked in comfortable silence, their hands twining together of their own accord. All too soon they reached the path that marked the entrance to her home.

"Thank you," she said as they slowed to a stop. "For everything."

"You're welcome," he answered, tugging her close.

She thought he was going to try and kiss her again, and

panic swirled. If he touched her she was pretty sure she wouldn't be able to say no. But instead he laid a soft peck on her forehead.

"For everything."

"All right, then. I'll see you around." She turned to go.

"Jessie?"

"What?"

"Can I see you again?"

She turned back to face him and said what she knew needed to be said. "I don't think that's a good idea."

"Why not?"

"Well, because we're competitors, for one. And I know you're still trying to get Goddess back from me—even if you won't admit it. Plus—and this is a doozy—your father is trying to put me out of business. He'd have kittens if he knew we were spending time together."

Nick smiled. "Actually, he expressly forbade it. But that doesn't mean I'm going to listen."

"I know, but…"

Nick grabbed her hands in his. "We're adults. We can do what we like. *I* don't want to put you out of business."

She shook her head. "You're forgetting I don't do relationships."

"Who said anything about a relationship? I don't do relationships either. I just want to go on a date with you."

"No, Nick. I'm sorry. I can't."

His mouth snapped closed and for a moment he just looked at her.

"What if I promised to show you a side of New York you've never seen? A place my father doesn't even know exists?"

Even though she knew it was a bad idea, she was intrigued. "Go on…"

"That's all I can tell you. But I promise you'll love it."

Although she hated to admit it, she was hooked. She wanted to know what he had in mind. Surely one night couldn't hurt? Maybe if they spent more time together she'd be able to get him out from under her skin.

"All right. One night. But then we're done."

He nodded sharply. "I'll take it. Pick you up tomorrow night at eight?"

"I'll be waiting. Is there a dress code?"

"Wear whatever makes you happy."

As soon as the words were out of his mouth he blew her a kiss and walked off into the night.

Jessie floated up the stairs to the apartment, humming under her breath. She dropped her coat and gloves on to a dining room chair, then glided into the kitchen in search of a glass of wine.

"You look a lot happier than you did the last time I saw you," her sister said.

"I am."

"Did Nick tell you what's going on?"

"He sure did."

"So what kind of wine are you getting?"

"White."

"It couldn't have been too bad, then."

"Actually, it was just about the worst," Jessie said, flopping down next to her sister on the couch.

"How so?"

"Nick's dad really is trying to close us down. He's the one who stole our employees and scared away our clients. Nick seems to think he won't stop until he puts us out of business."

Gloria stared at her, a horrified look on her face.

"So you're happy because…?"

"Because I'm going on a date with Nick."

"What?"

"You know—a date. Two people spending time together…"

"Yes, but *why*?"

"Oh, a lot of reasons," Jessie said, twirling her hair around her fingers.

"I've met walls who talk more than you. Name one reason why."

"He's promised to show me a side of New York I've never seen."

Gloria snickered. "I'll bet you ten dollars he means his bedroom."

"No, I don't think so. I've already told him we can't sleep together."

Her sister spat out her wine. "You did?"

"Yes."

"Who *are* you?"

"Your sister."

"No, you're not. My sister isn't afraid to sleep with a guy she finds attractive."

"Yes, but this is different. It's too risky. I just want to get to know him better."

"Oh. My. God."

"What?"

"You're in love."

"No way! I just like him. As a friend."

"Uh-uh. This is *not* how you act when you talk about your male friends. Deep down you want to marry him and have five babies and a little white dog." Her sister laughed. "Figures you'd fall for the guy who could ruin everything you've worked for."

Jessie threw one of the worn green pillows at her. "I'm not in love and I'm never getting married. It's just one date. Then we're done."

Gloria tossed it back and bopped her on the head with another one for good measure.

"Enjoy it. Just remember who he is."

"The devil's son. I know. I won't forget. I promise."

But, she thought to herself, if you know you're going to end up in hell anyway, you might as well enjoy the ride.

CHAPTER SIX

"WAKE UP, SUNSHINE!" someone chirped, rudely interrupting the delicious dream she'd been having.

"Why is the bed shaking? Gloria, stop jumping on the bed!"

"Okay. But you should know that it's nine-thirty in the morning," Gloria said as she flopped down next to her.

"Nine-thirty?" Jessie opened her eyes and realized her room was already bright with sunshine. She must have forgotten to set her alarm. She waited for the usual sense of panic to set in, but it failed to make an appearance. She just felt exhausted.

"I suppose I should get up, huh?"

"I have a better idea."

Jessie flipped over so she could see Gloria.

"What?"

"I think we should take the day off."

The idea sounded surprisingly appealing. "But it's Thursday."

"Yep. It's the day that comes right after Wednesday."

"We have work to do," Jessie said, trying to convince herself as much as Gloria.

"I know. But you've been working nonstop for the last year and a half. When was the last time you took a day off?"

Jessie thought for a minute. Surely it couldn't have been that long. "Becky's wedding?"

"Yep. Becky's wedding. That was three months ago."

That would explain why she felt so tired. Still, there was no time.

"But there's the Goddess campaign to get done and a creative team to replace. I don't have time to take a day off."

Gloria sighed. "Jessie, your alarm beeped for thirty minutes straight. You never heard it. I had to come in here and turn it off. *That's* how tired you are."

Wow. Okay, maybe Gloria had a point.

"What would we do on this mythical day off?"

"Get a massage? Take a yoga class? Eat too much chocolate?"

Every muscle in her body screamed at her to agree. "It's tempting to say yes."

"Then say yes." Gloria frowned at her. "I hate to say this, but if you don't start taking better care of yourself you're not going to be around to see all your hard work pay off."

Gloria was right, she knew. She deserved to take a little time for herself. Roar could live without her for one day.

"All right, you're on. Can you schedule us massages while I go take a quick shower?"

"You got it."

Gloria bounced up and headed in the direction of the kitchen. Jessie got up a little more slowly, then shuffled into the bathroom that had been her one extravagance when remodeling the old brownstone. It was all colored glass and dark hardwoods, and it made her feel like a fairy princess every time she walked in the door. She turned on the waterfall in her oversized shower and let it flow in a river over her back.

Opening her eyes, she saw the waterproof card she kept in the shower to remind her to do monthly breast examinations. Sighing, she decided there was no time like the present.

She began moving the pads of her fingers in a circular pattern around her breast, trying not to hold her breath. She was young. Chances were she wouldn't find anything. Just because her mother had died of breast cancer it didn't mean she was doomed. She finished her inspection of her left breast and moved on to the right side. Halfway done and no bad news.

She allowed herself to relax a little as she fell into a rhythm. Press, move. Press, move. Press…wait. What was that? Jessie kneaded at the spot a little more, trying to feel the edges of the knot. That definitely didn't feel right. Quickly she felt the same place on her other breast. There was nothing there. She moved back and poked around some more, not wanting to admit to herself what she'd found.

A lump. Cancer.

Her brain flooded with images of her mother after her diagnosis. Trying to look brave as she put a hat on her balding head. Throwing up in the bathroom. Wasting away in a hospital bed.

She couldn't have cancer. She just couldn't.

A low keening echoed around the tile room and after a moment Jessie realized it was her. Giving in to the pain and fear crashing in her brain, she slid down the wall and curled up on the bottom of the shower, sobbing.

"Jessie? Jessie, what's going on? Are you okay in there?"

Jessie tried to answer, but her voice failed her.

A few seconds later Gloria crashed through the door. "Jessie?"

"I'm here," Jessie croaked from her place on the shower floor.

Panic and worry flashed across Gloria's pale face as she crossed the room and reached in to shut off the water.

"What are you doing? Why are you curled up on the floor? Jessie, you're shaking like a leaf!"

This was not news. The water had turned cold ages ago, but she hadn't had the energy to turn it off. Instead she'd just curled tighter around herself, waiting for the sobbing to stop. It still hadn't.

Gloria grabbed a towel off the rack and went to her knees on the damp shower floor so she could cocoon Jessie in its fluffy softness.

"What's wrong, Jessie?" she asked, gently rubbing the tears off her face.

"I—I found a lump. In my breast. Gloria, I have c-c-cancer!"

"You found what? Are you sure? Let me feel."

Jessie grabbed her hand and moved it to the place where she'd felt the knot. "Here."

Gloria kneaded for a second.

"You're right. This doesn't feel right. But that doesn't mean it's cancer."

"Of course it is."

"No. I've read that, like, eight out of ten lumps are benign. It's probably nothing."

"But Mom…"

"But nothing. Just because Mom got breast cancer doesn't mean we will."

"But what if it is?" Jessie asked, hating how weak her voice sounded.

"Then we'll deal with it. You're not going to die," her sister said, eyes sparking with anger. "You're not—do you hear me?"

Jessie nodded slowly, not believing her but knowing she had to pull it together. For her sister's sake.

"Deal with it. Right. Of course. I need to make an appointment."

"Yes, you do. But first you need to get dressed. And then we're going to go get those massages. Because you won't get a mammogram appointment straight away and right now you need to relax," she said, grabbing Jessie's arms and helping her up.

Jessie made herself smile. "All right, boss. Give me ten minutes and I'll be ready."

* * *

By the time they sat down to eat at the vegetarian restaurant attached to the spa Jessie felt a little more hopeful. Even if it was cancer, treatment had come a long way in the fifteen years since her mom had died. She could probably kick it in nothing flat. And, since she'd always looked good in hats, chemotherapy fashion wouldn't be a problem.

"Stop it," Gloria said.

She blinked. "Stop what?"

"Thinking about it."

"That's kind of a tall order. After all, it *does* signal the beginning of what could be a life-changing event."

"Or it could be nothing at all. You've got your appointment to see the doctor. Until then, don't think about it."

"I'll do my best," Jessie said, trying to smile. Of course that was easy for her sister to say. She wasn't the one who could be dying.

"I know what will distract you," Gloria said, taking a bite of her black bean and mango salad.

"What?"

"Shopping."

"I don't have anything I need to shop for. Unless you think I should stock up on hats now?"

"Nope, I'm not talking about things to cover your head with. I'm thinking about things to cover your naughty bits with."

"Lingerie? Why? I've got a whole drawerful."

"Yes, but you have a hot date tonight. Why not find something that will make you feel sexy?"

In all the drama she'd actually forgotten about her date with Nick. For a moment she thought about canceling, but something deep in her gut rebelled at the idea. If she was dying, she deserved to have a little fun before she went.

Her decision made, she nodded at her sister.

"I've got plenty of cute underwear. But I guess one more

set wouldn't hurt—as long as it matches the new outfit I'm about to buy."

Gloria clapped her hands. "That's the spirit. Where to?"

"Well, he said to wear something that makes me happy. Which means…"

"Sparkles. Lots and lots of sparkles. All right, sis. Let's find you something that sparkles brighter than the sun."

Jessie grinned and they set off, arm in arm. Cancer could wait. She had shopping to do.

"How beautiful! Are those for me?" Jessie asked as she opened the door and noticed the bouquet of tulips in Nick's outstretched hand.

"Of course. I thought they might put you in the proper frame of mind for our date."

"Oh, really? Trying to butter me up so you can get me into bed?"

To his credit, Nick did not look at all embarrassed. "Well, my bedroom *is* one part of New York you've never seen."

She groaned. "Gloria, I owe you ten dollars!" she shouted.

"Told you so," called a muffled voice from somewhere inside the big house.

Nick raised an eyebrow at her. "What was that about?"

"When I told her we were going out tonight that's exactly what she said. About your bedroom."

"Oh. *Damn.* I hate to be predictable."

Jessie gave his outfit a closer look. He was wearing a black motorcycle jacket, faded denim jeans, and sturdy black boots. It should have looked ridiculous on him, but it didn't. In fact, he looked completely delicious.

"Well, *that* is not what I thought you'd be wearing when you showed up. So score two points for originality."

"And do you like what you see?" he asked, grinning evilly.

"I'd tell you, but your ego's already big enough. I'm going to go put these in water, and then we can go."

She needed a moment alone to center herself. Nick *did* look good but, more than that, his presence made her heart thunder in a way she wasn't ready for. She had no problem with their physical attraction. In fact after this morning's discovery she had decided to let the evening end in whatever way felt right—even if it led to his bedroom. But her heart was more off-limits than ever. She was not going to let herself become dependent on someone when so much was on the line.

One step at a time, she told herself as she put the tulips in a funky metal vase. It was just a date. No different than the hundreds of other dates she'd been on over the years. She'd have a good time, hop into his bed—and hop back out in the morning, just like she always did.

She pasted a cheerful smile on her face and put a swagger in her hips as she stepped back into the entranceway where she'd left him. When she saw his eyes slowly wander down her body she knew she'd chosen the right outfit. The shimmery copper top slithered perfectly over her thin torso, stopping just below the top button of her dark denim skinny jeans—which also had a sparkly sheen. On her feet were her favorite black stilettos—the ones that made her four inches taller. She felt amazing.

"Like what you see?" she asked, in the same teasing tone he'd used.

"You have no idea how much."

The first stirrings of desire fizzed in her veins. "Maybe you can show me later. But I want to see what you've got planned for me first."

"Then let's get on our way," he said, opening the door. "I have a big evening planned."

* * *

Nick smiled when he saw Jessie's mouth drop open at the sight of their ride for the evening.

"Where's Bob?"

"I gave him the night off. To show you this side of New York I need to be in the driver's seat."

"Well, all right." She ran her hand along the sleek hood of the cherry-red luxury sports car he'd rented. "So far I approve of your taste."

"I thought you would," he murmured as he held the door open for her.

"Are you going to tell me where we're going?"

"Nope. Just sit back and enjoy the ride. I've even got some of your favorite tunes cued up."

She laughed as one of her favorite eighties songs started playing. "Good job, you." Within seconds her toe was tapping. Then she started humming, apparently not even aware of what she was doing.

God, she was adorable. "You can sing if you want."

"What?"

"Sing. To the radio. It's obvious you want to."

She grinned sheepishly. "Really?"

"Really."

"All right—but remember you asked for it."

He nodded and she let loose, belting out the familiar words in a voice fit for Broadway. He grinned and settled back into the leather seat, enjoying the way the powerful car responded to his touch—and hoping Jessie might do the same later on.

All too soon they arrived at their destination. He pulled into the dark parking garage, into his reserved parking space.

"Ready?" he asked as he turned the car off. She looked around, apparently confused.

"Wait. We're really going to your apartment?"

"No."

"But this is…"

"Just wait and see!"

He helped her out of the car and led her over to his private elevator. The door opened after he punched in his security code and he let her in first, blocking the number pad so she couldn't tell which floor they were going to. But he couldn't help the grin that emerged as the numbers kept ticking higher.

"You *are* pleased with yourself, aren't you?" she said, eyeing him critically.

"Sure am."

"Hmm. I'm going to assume there's a good reason for that."

At long last the elevator dinged, signaling they had arrived.

"After you."

She stepped hesitantly out on to the rooftop. "What are we…?" Then she spotted it. "A helicopter? Are you taking me on a *helicopter* ride?"

"You better believe it. You said you love how New York sparkles at night. But you can't fully appreciate how many lights there are until you see them from the sky."

She looked at him silently and for a moment he thought she might cry. Had he done something wrong? But then she was throwing her arms around his neck and hugging him for all she was worth.

"You, Nick Thornton, are an amazing man."

Shaken by the power of her response, Nick fell back on the humor that had always been his savior. "Save those words until you really mean them, sweetheart…after I've gotten you in bed."

His words had exactly the effect he wanted. She bounced back on her heels, trying to decide whether or not to be miffed, but definitely out of kissing range.

"You're also a scoundrel. Now, take me up in the sky. Is this thing yours?"

"Yep. My grandfather bought it for me for my twenty-first birthday. I suppose he knew I'd need a reliable way to get away from my dad—quickly."

She laughed. "Sounds like my kind of guy, your grand-father."

"Yes, he would have liked you. Let's go!"

Jessie looked around her in amazement. She'd never seen New York like this. The city stretched below her as far as the eye could see. From this distance the busy streets looked like rivers of light, and the buildings twinkled with every color imaginable.

"It's beautiful," she said through the headset that connected her to the man next to her.

He turned and grinned. "It is, isn't it? *This* is New York at its best."

The chopper turned and a moment later she saw the Statue of Liberty, glowing proudly in the harbor.

"You know, I've never actually been there—to see her," Jessie said, pointing.

"Then let's take a closer look."

Soon they were flying across the harbor, swooping around the famous statue as close as they dared.

"I feel like a bird," Jessie said, loving the way the chopper could turn on a dime.

"That's one of the things I love about flying too," Nick said. "There's also something about the insanity of it. A little over a hundred years ago flying hadn't even been invented yet."

Jessie looked at him, taking note of the quiet confidence that radiated from him. He looked like a man who was used to winning. Part of her wondered if this was all just part of some elaborate plot to get her to agree to sell Roar.

But when he grinned at her all she saw was joy. Surely he wasn't that good an actor?

"Want to take one more spin around the city?"

"Yes, please!"

She applied herself to the view again, thinking about all the lives those sparkling lights represented. What would her mother have said if she had seen this? If she'd met Nick? Probably something like, *Don't let this one go, sweetheart. This one knows how to live.*

But she knew she'd have to let him go—sooner rather than later. Much better to keep things simple and get out before hearts got broken.

"Penny for your thoughts?" he said.

"Oh, just thinking about how much my mom would have loved this."

"Well, I'll bet she'd be just as glad that *you're* getting to enjoy it."

"You're right." But she didn't want to talk about her mother with him, so she decided to change the subject. "You know, I've never heard you talk about *your* mom. Where is she?"

He shrugged. "Right now? I don't know. Probably quietly getting drunk at some required social function. I haven't talked to her in months."

"That's sad. How come?"

He looked out the window so she couldn't see his expression. But his voice sounded sad even through her headphones. "Because she was more of a birth parent than a real mother. I was raised by nannies. When I refused to marry the girl she had picked out she pretty much washed her hands of me."

"And what kind of girl was that?" she couldn't help but ask.

"The kind that looked great in a cocktail gown, ran parties like a dream, and who was only interested in the kind of sparkle that you buy at a jewelry store."

The kind that had been a dime a dozen at the charity ball they'd gone to together. She made a face. "Not your kind of woman at all, huh?"

"You've got that right."

"Is that the kind of woman you're still expected to marry?"

"Yes. Good thing I have no plans to ever leave bachelorhood behind."

"I see."

In other words they were on the same page. She could enjoy him tonight without worrying that he would want more. So why did she feel so disappointed?

Her ears filled with the thudding whir of the rotors and she gave herself to the beauty below her.

"Are you getting hungry yet?" he asked eventually.

As soon as Jessie thought about it her stomach growled. "Starved."

He grinned. "Good."

Soon he was setting the chopper gently down. Not on a rooftop, as she had expected, but on the deck of a huge yacht anchored in the harbor.

"Is this yours, too?" she gasped.

"No, it belongs to a friend. But I thought this was probably another side of New York you've never seen. It's my second favorite view."

Too amazed to come up with a witty response, she just nodded.

"Sit tight. I'll come around and help you down. It's a bit tricky."

A minute later he appeared at her door, holding out his hand. She took it and put her foot on the step, expecting to float gracefully down. Instead her stiletto caught in a metal rut and she tumbled forward into his arms.

"Thanks for catching me," she said when she'd caught her breath, grinning up at him.

"Thanks for throwing yourself at me. It's got my appetite revving."

She laughed when he grabbed her butt and squeezed.

"I hate to tell you this, but my derrière is *not* on the dinner menu."

"Perhaps for dessert, then," he said, reluctantly releasing his hold.

"We'll see. Where are we eating? Did you transport a restaurant into the middle of the harbor?"

"Good question. Shall I show you to our table?" he asked, offering her his arm.

"Yes, please."

He led her down a short metal stairway on to a wooden deck. "This is what we call the promenade. Your dinner is waiting just through here," he said, leading her around the side of the boat.

What she saw on the other side made her gasp out loud. There was a table set for two with fine china, real silver, and crystal wine glasses. A tuxedoed waiter stood off to one side.

"You did all this for me?"

He smiled. "Of course. I'd do just about anything to make a beautiful woman like you happy."

Not *I'd do anything to make* you *happy*, she noticed. Just a beautiful woman *like* her. She wondered how often he had pulled this trick. But then, remembering he'd been in London for the last few years, she realized it couldn't have been too terribly often. She shook her head silently at herself, deciding that, whether this was something unique he'd done just for her or not, she fully intended to enjoy the experience. After all, a tiny voice in her head said, she might not get another chance.

"This is wonderful, Nick. Thank you."

He nodded and pulled her chair out for her. "Let's eat, shall we?"

The waiter went into action as she sat, pouring golden liquid into her glass. "Champagne?" she asked.

"Of course. I remember how bubbles go to your head."

"They do at that. Plus, it's the only wine fitting for a celebration—which is what this is," Jessie said.

"What are we celebrating?"

"Life. It's too short. We need to enjoy it while it lasts."

"I'll drink to that," Nick replied, tipping his glass to clink it on hers.

Jessie looked into his eyes and almost drowned in the depths she saw there. She felt the cage of self-control she kept around her heart crack open the tiniest bit. As soon as the thought occurred to her she slammed it back closed. This could never be more than a one-night stand. Neither one of them did long-term.

The waiter brought out course after course after course of delicious food as they talked about anything and nothing. Caviar. Delicate salads. Pâté. Filets. By the time the waiter took their final plates away and disappeared Jessie thought her stomach might burst.

"I can't believe I ate all that."

"I'm glad you did. I can't stand bird-like eaters."

"Well, then, you should keep me around. I never met a food I didn't like to eat."

He threw her a wicked smile. "Oh, I intend to. At least for the night."

Again, she found herself feeling disgruntled. She didn't like the fact that he thought getting her naked was a done deal. She wasn't *that* easy. It was time he realized it.

"I don't think so," she blurted.

"You don't think so, what?"

"I don't think I'll be staying the night."

"Y-You won't?"

"Nope," she said, almost unable to keep a straight face. She loved turning the tables on him.

"Why?" He seemed genuinely bewildered.

"Because you seem to expect that I will. And if that's what all this," she said, motioning wildly at their surroundings, "was about, then accepting your invitation would make me no better than a prostitute."

"How on earth did you arrive at *that* conclusion?"

"Because you've been trying to buy my affections. And, as I told you before, I am not for sale."

"Are you serious?"

Was she? She wasn't sure. "As a heart attack," she said. Okay, apparently she was.

"So if I was to do this," he said, getting out of his chair and kneeling in front of her, "and beg you to stay, would you still refuse?"

"*Are* you begging?" she asked, doing her best not to let him see how much his closeness affected her.

Instead of answering he gently pulled her left hand from where it had been sitting frozen in her lap and started kissing a path up her arm. Her breath stuttered when he reached the inside of her elbow, igniting every nerve in her body with one strategically placed kiss. Then he kissed his way back down to her palm, every touch of his soft mouth feeding the fire.

When he got to her fingertips he looked up, his eyes dark with longing. "Please. Stay."

Say yes, her body screamed. But she couldn't give in. He wasn't begging yet. "I can't."

"Please. I'm begging."

There they were. The magic words. She looked at the powerful man she'd brought to his knees and felt a strange sort of pride. This man could have any woman he wanted, but he wanted *her*. Was begging *her*.

"And if I say yes now, what happens in the morning?"

His mouth rose up into a slow, sexy grin. "I'll bring you breakfast in bed, if you want. Or take you to brunch at the Four Seasons. Hell, I'll sail us to Nassau for lunch if that's what you want. Just say yes."

Triumph raced through her. "I'm still not sure. Kiss me."

"As you wish," he said.

He circled his arms around her and lifted her bodily off her chair, then lowered her until she straddled his lap.

"You," he breathed, "are amazing. I want to kiss every inch of you—from these luscious lips," he said, breaking off to suck her bottom lip, "to these…" His hand moved to the crotch of her jeans and slowly rubbed her most sensitive area.

She groaned, fighting the urge to thrust more of herself into his inquisitive hand. She knew that there was a big chance she'd regret this later, but as he kissed the pulsepoint in her neck she realized she no longer cared.

Life was short. She deserved to know what a night with a man like this would be like.

Waving goodbye to her principles, she wrapped her legs around his waist, bringing her sex into contact with his hard length, separated only by their clothing.

"Okay. I'll stay."

"Thank you. I promise you won't regret it."

"Talk is cheap, buddy," she managed to say as he slid his hand under her shirt. "Prove it."

Taking that as the invitation it was, he picked her up and carried her into the cabin below, locking the doors behind them.

The bedroom, she noted as he kicked the door closed, was surprisingly posh. The walls were a deep crimson. The floor an expensive-looking hardwood. And the bed was gigantic, and covered with a mountain of pillows and satin sheets.

"Up you go," Nick said, throwing her on the bed.

She was so intent on the hard body above her she barely registered the change in position. Her hands scrabbled on his white button-down shirt, desperate to feel the planes of his chest.

"You first," he said, pulling upward on her top. It vanished over her head, exposing the gorgeous copper bra she'd bought to match it. "Good God, you're beautiful," he whispered.

Without waiting for permission, he tugged her jeans down over her thighs. He got frustrated when the cuffs caught on her heels, but when she brought one leg up, intending to take her shoe off herself, he growled.

"No. I want them on."

Jessie melted at the command in his voice. He delicately maneuvered first one jean leg, then the other, over her shoes, trying to be delicate. When it didn't work, he just yanked until her pants ripped.

"Hey!" she squawked.

"Don't worry. I can buy you more."

She knew she should be offended by that. Should, in fact, demand that he unhand her and head out the door. But when she saw the blissed-out expression on his face she couldn't make herself move.

For a long moment he just stared, his gaze moving from her red curls to the mounds of her breasts, down to the auburn curls peeking out from the copper lace undies, and then down to the stilettos she was still wearing.

"You are my teenage daydream come to life."

Jessie shivered at the raw heat in his voice. "Oh, yeah? Well, what would you have wanted to do with the girl of your dreams?"

"All sorts of things," he whispered.

"Show me."

He grinned at her, then nodded.

Without warning, he dived down low, taking the entirety of her nether lips into his mouth, his tongue looking for entry through the delicate lace. Her hips reared up off the bed of their own accord, seeking something more.

He rumbled appreciatively, then shoved the lace of her panties aside and delicately stroked her with his tongue, licking and sucking at the sensitive tissues. When at long last he found the hard little nub at her center she thought she might die. She'd had a lot of men, but none had paid as much attention to her as this.

Her ability to think disappeared—along with the voice that begged her to maintain some semblance of control. She felt her hips rocking back and forth. Knew her back was arching, begging for more.

"Do you want me, baby?" he asked, his fingers teasing all the places his tongue had been.

"Oh, yes. So much."

"Good," he growled, "because I want you."

"Make love to me, Nick," she said, in a breathy voice she didn't recognize.

"I thought you'd never ask," he said, and suddenly his hand was gone.

She whimpered in frustration.

"Oh, I see. You want to come before I do, huh?"

She could only nod, her eyes still pressed tightly closed.

"Look at me," he commanded.

Slowly she opened her eyes.

"Beg me."

For a moment she just stared at him. She didn't beg. *Ever.* But then he rubbed his thumb over her and her pride crumbled.

"Please, Nick," she whimpered. "Please."

"Please what?"

"Please make me come."

"Your wish," he said, thrusting his fingers in and out, "is my command."

Unable to help herself, Jessie locked her legs around his waist and gave herself over to the sensations. Losing herself in the motion of his hand, she climaxed in record time.

She came back to herself an indeterminate time later and registered Nick hovering over her, his breath harsh with want.

"I need to feel you inside me, Nick," she said, unable to think of anything more eloquent.

He groaned, then ripped his shirt off his body with one hand. She fumbled with the slippery metal button on his jeans, desperate to feel him inside her. Seconds later he took over, pulling down his jeans and the boxer briefs underneath them in one fell swoop.

She heard the rip of a condom package, then seconds later Nick was back, nudging at her entrance.

"Ready, baby?"

"Oh, yes." She thrust her hips upward.

He sank into her up to the hilt and they both groaned. It felt as if he belonged there.

She whimpered and shivered, no longer able to form words. Luckily he knew what she wanted, and soon he was moving in and out, in and out, somehow hitting the sensitive bundle of nerves inside her with every stroke.

She knew she should try and take some control back, but instead she just grabbed for his back.

"More!" she cried. "More."

He complied, thrusting even harder into her core. She threw her head back and closed her eyes, loving how he played her body. Seconds later her orgasm began to build, rising in intensity until she thought she might break. When his thumb delicately began to massage her she broke into a thousand pieces of infinite pleasure.

She was still shivering with aftershocks when he began

to move with more intensity. She wrapped her legs around him, determined to take control and give him the pleasure he deserved, but before she knew it she was shattering again.

This time he came with her. The pair of them shuddered together in silence, enjoying the aftershocks.

Finally he turned to her and said, "Jessie, don't ever leave me."

Looking into his deep blue eyes, she found herself wishing she could actually promise him eternity. Instead she whispered, "I won't. At least not until after you feed me breakfast."

He laughed. "Where shall it be? In bed or at the Four Seasons?"

"How about Tahiti?"

"You're on. I'll just have to tell the boat captain in the morning."

"Okay," she murmured. "But you'll probably have to make love to me another time or two before then."

"Don't worry. If I have my way you're not going to get any sleep at all."

She just smiled and kissed him. This was one sleepless night she was looking forward to.

CHAPTER SEVEN

IN THE MOMENTS before Jessie opened her eyes she was disconcerted by a feeling that her bed was rocking. Surely she hadn't had that much to drink last night? When she reached out her arms in a tentative stretch her right hand hit something solid. And warm.

Her eyes snapped open as full consciousness returned—and with it memories of the night's festivities. Nick had made love to her three more times before they'd finally fallen into an exhausted slumber. It had been an amazing sexual experience. Usually she was in charge, taking exactly what she wanted from the men she slept with. But last night Nick had been in complete control…and she'd loved it.

But now it was morning. Time to get back to work and take charge of the mess that was currently her life. Looking down at the sleekly muscled body of the beautiful man next to her, she sighed. It was too bad he was a Thornton. The events of last night could never be repeated—no matter how much she might wish otherwise.

Nick stirred and stretched, giving her a sleepy smile. "Morning, beautiful."

"Good morning."

"What's the matter? You look worried."

"Just thinking about everything I need to do today, that's all."

"I thought we were going to Tahiti today," he said, drawing her down on the pillow next to him. "But if you want we could stay right here."

Twining her red hair in his fists, he pulled her close and

kissed her none too gently. Desire flared as instantly as if someone had flipped a switch and she yielded, losing herself in the teasing heat of his lips and tongue. But when he reached down to cup her butt she pulled back.

Making love with him again would be sheer folly. Living for the moment was all well and good, but their moment was over.

As if on cue, her phone buzzed.

"Mmmph," she said, dragging her lips away from his. "I've got to get this."

"No, don't…" he protested.

But she moved quickly out of his reach, searching for her phone. She saw it peeking out of the back pocket of her jeans, which were draped over a lamp on the dresser. She dove, but by the time she wrestled it out it had stopped ringing.

"Damn it." It had been her doctor's office. Too impatient to wait to hear what the message said, Jessie punched the button that would call them back.

"Dr. Davies's office."

"Hi, this is Jessie. Jessie Owens," she said, turning away from the bed so Nick couldn't see her face.

"Oh, hi, Jessie! Listen, we can get you in sooner at nine-thirty this morning. Can you make it?"

"What time is it now?"

"Eight-fifteen."

"Um, can you hold on a second?"

"Sure."

"Nick, where are we?"

"On our way to Tahiti," he teased.

"No, really. This is serious. Where *are* we?"

"Close to Battery Park."

She did the math in her head. If she got out of here in the next ten minutes, and the subway was running on time…

"Yes, I can make it."

"Great, I'll pencil you in. See you soon!"

Jessie pushed the "end" button and took a deep breath. "Nick, I'm sorry, but I've got to go."

"Go where?"

"I'd rather not tell you. It's kind of personal," she said, not wanting to trust him with her secret.

His face darkened. "Okay, if that's the way you want to play it. You're just going to run out on me, huh?"

"No, that's not it at all," she said, even though she knew she should just act tough and put this—whatever "this" was—to an end. "I've got an appointment in a little over an hour that I really can't miss. It's sort of an emergency."

His expression lightened a little bit. "Where is it?"

When she told him, he shook his head. "There's no way you'll make it there on time if you're planning on taking the subway. Let me call Bob. He'll drive you."

"That's really not necessary," she said, worried that Bob would tell Nick what their final destination was.

"Nonsense. I insist. You take a shower—I'll call Bob."

Deciding to think of her chauffeur-driven ride to the doctor as the final scene in their short-lived romance, she nodded. She didn't have time to fight with him.

"Where's the shower?"

She was still tying her wet hair into a bun when Nick hustled her off of the yacht. The marina where it had docked was beautiful. Although she could see they were just blocks away from the financial district, it seemed to be in another world. Gargantuan boats rocked on gentle waves, bumping into the weathered wood of the boardwalk. Great old trees rustled overhead, inviting all who saw them to sit a while under their shade.

"This is amazing."

He shrugged. "I guess… You're welcome to come back and admire the view anytime."

"I thought you said you had borrowed a friend's boat?"

"I did. About two and a half months ago. I'll give it back when I find somewhere better to live."

"You *live* on here?"

"For now. Although I'd prefer my permanent home to be a bit less rocky, you know?"

"I guess," she said, not trusting herself to say more.

It was just more proof that he was out of her league. He lived on a yacht—she lived in a brownstone that she could only afford because she'd inherited it from her mother. Otherwise she'd be another young professional Manhattanite sharing a studio apartment with two other roommates. Good thing they both knew this had no future.

Still, when at long last they made their way to the parking lot and the limo that awaited her, she couldn't resist leaning in for one last kiss.

"Thanks," she whispered against his lips, "for everything. You sure know how to show a girl a good time."

He smiled, a strange glint shining in his eye. "You're welcome—but you're not off the hook yet."

"What do you mean?"

"You promised you'd stay till after breakfast. I haven't eaten yet, so…"

She glanced down at her phone. Eight-forty-five. She had to hit the road. "How about dinner instead? I'll text you."

He nodded. "You better."

She saluted and got into the waiting car, already cursing herself for making another date with him. When it came to Nick, her brain seemed to be permanently short-circuited.

But it was just dinner. No reason it had to lead to more. And it wouldn't. She was almost positive that she could resist him.

Jessie tried not to fidget in the plastic chair. Why did doctors' offices always have to be so uncomfortable? If she ran a place like this the waiting area would be furnished with velvet sofas, flowery pillows, and chenille throw blankets you could cover up with when you got cold. That way patients wouldn't get grumpy when forced to wait for an hour after their mammogram to find out if they had cancer.

"Jessica Owens?"

Jessie grabbed her purse and coat, then followed the woman in pink scrubs out of the waiting room. They walked down a long carpeted hallway, past all the exam rooms, into a lushly furnished office. Uh-oh. This couldn't be good.

"Jessie, sorry to keep you waiting out there so long. Please sit," her doctor said.

She took a deep breath and settled herself in one of the wooden chairs that sat in front of the desk. "What have you got for me, Doc? Was the lump just a figment of my imagination?"

The gray-haired woman sighed and leaned forward, resting her hands in front of her on the desktop. "You know that's what I want to tell you, Jessie. But unfortunately the lump is real."

"Is it cancer, Dr. Davies?" she whispered.

Her world started to shatter.

Her doctor turned her computer monitor so Jessie could see the mammography image on her screen.

"This is your right breast. The one where you felt the lump. See this here?" She pointed at a bright white circle with white lines snaking off it. "That's what we're dealing with. It's highly suspicious, and given your family history I'd like to skip the less accurate tests and get you in for a biopsy right away."

No doubt about it. This was the end.

"So I have cancer."

"We can't be sure of that yet. That's why I want to do

the biopsy. We can get it done today, and by Monday we'll know what we're dealing with."

Jessie ordered herself to ignore the gibbering panic shrieking in her brain and pay attention. "A biopsy?"

"Yes, but don't worry. It's a simple procedure and we can do it right here in the office. You probably won't feel much like going into work afterward though. Can you take the day off?"

Jessie thought about the mountain of work that waited for her at the office. She was supposed to present an entire campaign to a client in two weeks. And, since she'd just lost her lead creative team, she was going to have to do it herself. No, she really couldn't afford to take another day off. But she realized she didn't really care. If she was dying of cancer it wouldn't matter anyway.

"Yes, that's not a problem. I just have to let my sister know."

How was she going to tell her sister? Gloria had been even more devastated than she had when their mother had died. And Jessie had promised her she'd never leave her. What would Gloria say when she found out she had lied?

Dr. Davies got up from her desk and came to sit in the chair next to her.

"Jessie?"

Her voice sounded very far away. Jessie had to force herself to answer. "Yes?"

Dr. Davies grabbed her hand and squeezed. "Everything's going to be okay."

Suddenly anger flared to life. She couldn't promise that. "How can you say that? You treated my mother. You *know* what happened."

Dr. Davies shook her head. "You are not your mother. This is not the same situation. By the time your mom came to me it was already too late. She waited too long. But you came in as soon as you noticed something. Even if it is cancer it's early days. And treatment has come a very long way in the last fifteen years. You're going to be all right."

Jessie wanted so badly to believe her. "Promise?"

Her doctor looked uncomfortable. "For legal reasons, I can't make promises. But I believe with all my heart that it's true."

"Okay. That will have to be good enough." Jessie took a deep breath and squeezed the woman's hand. "Thank you."

Dr. Davies got up. "No problem. I'm going to go get that biopsy scheduled. Feel free to relax back here for a while. Oh, and when you talk to your sister ask her to come up here, okay? I don't want you going home alone."

Jessie nodded and powered up her phone.

Jessie was lying on an exam table, trying to convince herself to get up and get dressed, when she heard a welcome voice.

"Hey, doll," Gloria said. "They told me you're all done."

She opened her eyes a crack and rolled over onto her side—the side that hadn't just had a giant needle stuck in it. "That's what they tell me."

"You ready to get going, then? I brought you some clean clothes."

"I guess."

"You're going to have to get up."

"I know."

She didn't want to. Didn't want to have to go out into the world and try and pretend she was all right while she waited to hear if she was dying. She wasn't sure if she even could. It felt as if the world was ending.

Gloria tugged on her arm. "Come on, sis. Get up."

Jessie thought about refusing. What was the point? "Give me one good reason why I should."

Her sister tried to smile. "Because you can't eat a triple chocolate hot fudge sundae in a doctor's office."

"I don't know if I have the stomach for it."

Her sister was silent for a moment. When she continued Jessie could hear the tears in her voice.

"I need you to get up, Jessie. Please?"

That did the trick. As much as she was hurting, she couldn't stand to see her sister cry. "All right, I guess I can find room for some ice cream. Are you buying?"

Her sister nodded.

"All right, then." Forcing her body to move into a sitting position felt like one of the hardest things she'd ever done, but she did it. "Where are my clothes?"

Gloria smiled, clearly relieved, and threw a bag at her. "How embarrassing was it to have to do the walk of shame to your doctor's office?"

"Very. But it was totally worth it." Jessie's skin warmed at the memory of Nick's touch. It already seemed like something that happened a lifetime ago.

Gloria's jaw dropped. "Wow. You're blushing. You never blush. I'm going to need details."

Jessie shook her head. "Chocolate first. Details later."

"Fine. Just tell me one thing: are you going to see him again?"

Jessie smacked her head with her hand. "Oh, damn. I told him we could have dinner tonight. That sounds like an awful idea now!"

Gloria put her arm around Jessie's shoulders. "It might be just what you need. A distraction, you know?"

"I don't know…"

"Trust me. You'll feel a lot better after a roll in the hay or three. Now, get dressed, would you? I'll be waiting outside."

Then she turned and exited the exam room, humming a sexy song under her breath.

Jessie knew Gloria was right. If she was going to get through this weekend she was going to need to keep herself busy. *Very* busy. If she didn't…

Her mind gave her a sneak peek of what might be on repeat. She saw her mother pulling clumps of hair out of her head. Heard her dad's broken sobs after the doctor told him it was time to call in hospice care. Smelled the antiseptic that had been her mother's perfume those last few weeks.

Jessie stifled a sob. No way could she spend the entire weekend reliving those memories. If she did, she'd be ready to give up before she even got her diagnosis.

She needed to try and forget. Maybe even go somewhere she could escape. A vision of white sand and blue water shimmered in her mind's eye. Paradise. She needed to go to Paradise. And she needed to convince Nick to come with her. He would be an excellent distraction.

She opened the door and hurried out into the hallway.

"Gloria? Do you have Aunt Mimi's number in your phone? I think I'm going to take an impromptu trip to Paradise."

The bells on the restaurant door jingled. Nick looked up, hoping Jessie had arrived. But the harried-looking woman holding a pair of children by their hands was definitely not her. He scanned the restaurant from his seat in a brightly tiled booth, hoping she had snuck by him and was waiting in the bar or something.

No luck.

He tried not to worry. She wouldn't stand him up. Would she? When he stopped to think about it he didn't know her all that well. He knew what she looked like naked, and how brightly her eyes sparked when she was angry, but he had no idea how she would act in a relationship.

Not that this was a relationship. It was a fling, and that was all it could ever be. All he would *let* it be.

"Hi!"

Nick jumped. He'd forgotten where he was for a second, there. When Jessie's appearance registered, he grinned at the pink-nosed confection that had just sat down across from him.

"Hi, yourself! I didn't see you come in."

"Well, you know… With this red hair and my yellow coat I'm totally camouflaged."

Nick waved his hands at their gaudy surroundings. "Actually, this is one place you *do* blend in. I think your coat is the same color as that wall over there."

"You should see their margaritas. They're even brighter. Speaking of which…" Jessie waved. "Yoo-hoo, José!"

A man waved back and immediately made his way to their table.

"Jessie! How good to see you. You've been away too long!"

"Sorry, José. I've been working hard. Your new website is just about ready to go, though!"

José clapped his hands together. "I can't wait to see it. Tonight—whatever you want. It's on the house!"

"That's not necessary."

José squeezed her shoulder. "I know. But it's the least I can do. The marketing campaign you put together for us—it's magic!"

"In that case we'll have a round of margaritas. The big ones. And some chips and guacamole. Please."

"You got it," he said, and hurried off in the direction of the kitchen.

"A client of yours?" Nick asked.

"Not really. More of a charity case. They were about to go under and I couldn't stand to see that happen. They make the best chicken *mole* I've ever tasted."

Jessie smiled, but it didn't reach her eyes. She looked pale. And tired. There was a pinched look to her face that he didn't like.

"Are you okay?"

She nodded. "Oh, I'm fine. Just a tough day."

"More of my father's shenanigans?" The thought made his blood boil.

"No, no. Not him. It's personal stuff."

"The same personal stuff that had you rushing off this morning?"

She shrugged her shoulders. "Sort of."

Nick was about to pry further when José slammed the cocktails down. The two dinner-plate-sized margarita glasses filled with sunset-colored layers covered most of the space between them.

"Wow."

"Wait till you taste it."

He pulled his drink toward him and took a cautious sip from the salt-covered rim. He'd expected it to be sickly sweet, but instead the perfect combination of tart citrus and tequila tickled his tastebuds.

"This is fantastic!"

"I know. These guys are national treasures." She kicked back, putting her feet up on the bench next to him. "Just close your eyes and pretend you're at the beach."

He grabbed her feet and put them in his lap, neatly tossing her ballet flats on to the floor before applying his thumbs to her soles. "In that case, feel free to imagine I'm the cabana boy the resort has sent to see to your every whim."

This time the grin lit up her entire face. "Oh, I tend to have a lot of whims. I prefer not to pay for most of them, though."

"This cabana boy has happily volunteered his time."

"In that case, I think I'll have a little fun."

Jessie slid a little further down in the booth, wiggling her feet until her toes touched the rapidly lengthening bulge in his jeans. He took a sharp breath in, not sure whether he should encourage her or stop her.

Before he could decide, José arrived again. "Your guacamole. Jessie, I made sure to put an extra squirt of lime juice in it, so it should be just the way you like it."

"You're a mind-reader, José. Thank you."

He smiled at her, his eyes soft. José wanted her—no doubt about it. But Nick could hardly blame him.

"Should we have some of that chicken *mole* you were telling me about, Jessie?"

Jessie nodded. "Yep. Oh, and José? Can you bring some of those *quesadillas* I love so much?"

"Of course," he answered, bowing a little as he backed away from the table.

"José asked me to marry him, you know."

Jealousy roared to life in Nick's veins. "Really?"

"Yep. He said that with my marketing skills and his mama's cooking we could build an empire."

"*That's* why he wanted to marry you?"

"That and his mama wanted some redheaded grand-babies. They would have been pretty, with that caramel skin..."

"Uh-huh. And I'm sure it had nothing to do with him wanting to get you into bed."

She waved carelessly at him. "Oh, no. We've already been there, done that. Wasn't good enough to send a post-card home."

Nick couldn't help but laugh. "You are something else—you know that?"

"Something incredible?"

"Drink your margarita, Jessie."

She smiled and took a long drag on her straw. "What's your favorite beach?"

"I don't know that I have a favorite. I tend to like the ones that have palm trees and bikini-clad girls, though."

"That's too bad."

"You have a favorite, I take it?"

"Mmm-hmm. It's on an island in South Florida. The

sand is white, the water is blue, and at night you can see a galaxy's worth of stars."

"Sounds nice."

"It's more than nice. It's paradise. Would you like to go?"

"Absolutely. Anytime you want." A vacation alone with a mostly naked Jessie sounded like a fantastic idea.

She looked at him and smiled.

Their chicken *mole* and *quesadillas* arrived, along with another round of margaritas—this time on the rocks. He looked down at his glass and was shocked to see he'd actually finished his first one.

"Cheers," Jessie said, raising her new glass. He clinked his with hers, glad that at least this one was a little smaller.

"I made the toast last night. Now it's your turn."

"Oh…" He thought for a second. "To new adventures."

"I like that."

She went quiet and he applied himself to the food. It was delicious. Rich and tender with the perfect amount of spice.

"This is amazing. You did the right thing by saving them, Jessie."

"I know." He noticed she was toying with her food, not eating much.

"Is something wrong?"

"No. Just wondering… Are you busy this weekend?"

"Well, I should get some work done, but not particularly."

Although he did hope that he'd be spending at least one night with Jessie. Last night had merely whetted his appetite for her. It would take another romp or two to get her out of his system.

At least, he hoped that would do the trick.

"Will you come to Paradise with me?"

He felt his crotch twitch as desire coiled deep in his stomach. "I'd love to take you to paradise, baby. In fact, we can leave right now if you want."

She smiled. "That's not what I meant. I mean, yes, I totally want to get naked with you—but I want to take you to Paradise first. As in Paradise, Florida. My favorite beach."

He blinked. "You want to go to Florida? Tonight?"

"Yes." She bit her lip. "Actually, I already booked us plane tickets."

Nick shook his head, trying to wrap his head around the situation. He was usually the one surprising his date with a spontaneous trip. It felt odd to be on the receiving end.

"You bought plane tickets? When?"

"This afternoon."

"Why the sudden desire to go to Florida? And why do you want to go with me?"

"I like you. I like the beach. And it's been far too long since I saw the stars," she answered, looking everywhere but at him.

Nick saw the tension in her shoulders. The tightness of her jaw. And, if he wasn't mistaken, there were tears in her eyes. Something was wrong.

"I'm guessing there's more to it than that."

She shook her head. "Can you just let it go at that, Nick? I *need* to see the stars. And I don't want to go alone. Please come with me?"

Her voice cracked and he could tell she was having a hard time holding it together. He wanted to gather her in his arms and let her know that whatever it was it would be all right. But he couldn't promise that. So instead he grabbed her hand and kissed it.

"All right. Let's go to the beach."

She smiled, and the brightness of it took his breath away.

"Thank you, Nick." Then her smile faded. "I don't want you to get the wrong idea about this. About us."

He blinked. "What do you mean?"

"I'm not looking for a relationship. I want to spend the weekend together, but after that we can't be together."

Nick ignored the sharp pang in his stomach and smiled. "Don't worry, babe. We're on the same page there. One week is pretty much my max as far as relationships go."

Her shoulders sagged with relief. "Okay. Good. I just didn't want to lead you on."

"Don't worry about it." His brain kicked in, and he thought about what she'd said before. "Listen, I know you said you bought tickets, but wouldn't you rather take the Thornton plane? If I call the pilot he can be here in less than an hour."

She pulled back and shook her head. "No. This is my adventure. We're doing this my way. You, my friend, are flying commercial."

His phone trilled. Not sure whether he should be mad, or glad of the distraction, he picked it up and looked at the number.

"It's Bob."

She pulled her hand back and bounced up from the table. "Great! Now we can go!"

"Wait. How did you know he was on his way?"

"Oh, he gave me his number this morning, when he dropped me off. In case I ever needed a ride. So this afternoon I called him and asked him to help me surprise you. He thought it was a grand idea—he even volunteered to pack a suitcase for you."

Nick couldn't remember ever feeling so out-maneuvered. The better he got to know Jessie, the easier it was to understand how she'd made her agency so successful so fast. The woman was a force of nature.

Grinning, he got up from the table. "All right then, I guess we'd better be on our way! Paradise awaits!"

CHAPTER EIGHT

As Jessie inhaled the warm salt air through the open car windows she felt her body start to relax. This was what she needed. A couple of days here and she'd be ready for whatever the world could throw at her. Even cancer.

"Isn't this great?"

Nick glared at her from the passenger seat. His big body looked even larger in the minuscule space the compact car she'd rented offered its passengers. He was clearly uncomfortable.

"Next time you want to go on an adventure, I'm in charge of transportation."

"You've got a deal," she said, trying not to care that he thought there would be a next time.

Instead of examining the flutter in her heart, she concentrated on driving. The signs were hard to read in the dark, and she wasn't sure if she'd remember the turn-off. They had passed Shell Way, so Paradise Drive had to be... *there*! The wooden pelican that guarded the private road shone brightly in her headlights.

As she bumped down the sandy track the sky disappeared beneath a canopy of palm trees, leaving them in a tunnel of black.

"Are you sure this is the right way?" Nick asked.

"Positive. In fact..." The canopy dropped away, revealing the stilted beach house she loved. Although it looked a lot rougher around the edges than she remembered, its exterior was the same cheery pink. "We're here. Welcome to Paradise!"

"Thank goodness," he groaned, unfolding himself from the cramped space.

"The view is worth it, I promise," she said as she hopped out of the car.

Grabbing his hand, she pulled him past the house to the beach that waited on the other side. Seconds later the crashing of waves filled her ears and the sea wind blew through her hair.

Jessie found herself remembering the last time she'd been here. She and her mother had made the same race to the beach when they'd arrived. When they'd reached the surf, her mom had grabbed her hands and spun her in a circle.

"Isn't this amazing?" she'd shouted. "Jessie, this is what life is all about. I'm so glad to be here with you!"

That had been just two months before her mom had got her cancer diagnosis. Which meant it had been eating away at her at that very moment. Just as it was doing to *her* now.

Jessie couldn't bite back the sob that worked its way out of her throat. Life was so unfair. Why was this happening to her?

Nick walked up and put his arm around her shoulders. "Hey! What's wrong?"

Jessie tried to quiet the sobs, but couldn't get control. "I just… It's not fair… I miss her so much," she wailed.

"Oh, Jessie, I'm so sorry." Nick pulled her toward him until her head was resting against his chest. "You're talking about your mom, aren't you?"

Jessie nodded from her place inside his arms, letting his warmth chase away the pain. Her tears slowed, then stopped as he slowly swayed back and forth. Time stopped as she rested there, listening to his heartbeat, feeling strangely safe.

Eventually she forced herself to pull back. "Thank you," she said, unable to meet his eyes.

He gently pulled up on her chin. "No thanks necessary. I'm glad I was here for you."

His gaze was so tender the tears threatened to begin again. That would never do. She smiled and pulled away. "Ready for some star-gazing?"

He looked up at the sky. "Of course. That's what we came here to do, isn't it?"

"That's not real star-gazing." She pulled him down and gently pushed him backward until his head was pillowed on the sand. Then she flopped down next to him. "This is the only way to see them properly."

He sighed. "Ah. I see what you mean."

Jessie lost herself in the night sky as her body basked in the heat from the still sun-warmed sand. There were layers and layers of swirling stars, some shining brightly, some less so, and they combined to look like some sort of pepper-studded cosmic soup.

"Wow," Nick said.

"That's just about the only word for it."

"I've never seen so many stars. I had no idea there were so many."

"It makes you feel small, doesn't it?"

He nodded silently and reached for her hand.

"I used to sit out here with my mother, and we'd make up stories about all the things going on up there."

"What do you mean?" he asked, stroking her fingers.

"Well, when you see all those thousands and thousands of stars, doesn't it seem difficult to believe that ours is the only planet in the entire universe to have life on it?"

"I never really thought about it."

"We used to pick a star—any star. Like that one." She pointed up at the sky. "The bluish one over there to the left. And we'd spin stories about the people living on the planets around it. Sometimes they were blue, sometimes they had six legs, but usually they were people just like us, looking up at the sky, wondering what was out there."

Nick squeezed her hand. "She sounds like a wonderful woman."

"She was."

"And this house? It belongs to your family?"

"No. It belongs to a very dear friend of my mother's. I grew up calling her Aunt Mimi. We used to vacation here with her every spring, and in the fall we had it to ourselves for a week. I haven't been here since my mom died, but she's always telling me I'm welcome to use it any time."

"And is she here now?"

"No. It's just us. I called her this afternoon and she said she hasn't been down in a couple of months. And, according to Aunt Mimi, none of the neighbors are around either. Which means we can do something I've always wanted to do."

His teeth gleamed in the moonlight as he grinned. "Have sex on the beach?"

She shook her head. "Maybe later. Right now I want to go skinny-dipping."

"Skinny-dipping?"

"Yeah. Come on!"

She stood up and quickly stripped off her shirt and jeans. Nick didn't move.

"What are you waiting for?"

He pointed at her bra. "For you to be completely naked."

She thought about the bandage covering the needle marks from her biopsy. "I think I'll leave my bra on. Just in case somebody walks by."

"Chicken."

She snorted. "Said the man who's still fully clothed. Besides, I have every intention of taking my underwear off. No one can see my bottom half in the water. Are you coming with me?"

He frowned. "I haven't decided yet."

"Fine. But I'm taking these in the water with me," she said, cupping her breasts. Then she turned her back to him and slowly shimmied out of her thong underwear. "And if you want to get any closer to *this*," she said, caressing her butt, "you'll need to get off the beach."

She gave him one last meaningful look and then sprinted out into the surf, diving underneath the waves as soon as the water reached her upper thighs.

The shock of the cool water took her breath away. But soon her body adjusted and she reveled in the feeling of weightlessness.

She flipped on to her back and opened her eyes to stare at the heavens above. Floating like this, she could almost believe she was in space, one with the stars. For a moment she wondered if her mother was up there, looking down at her and wishing they could see each other again. She tried to imagine what her mom would say if she could see her now. Probably something like, *Stop star-gazing and go pay attention to that man meat you brought with you.*

Just then strong arms circled her waist and shoulders, and she jumped. "Nick, that better be you…"

"It is," he rumbled in her ear. "Although I can pretend to be someone else if you like."

She pretended to think about it while her heart-rate settled down. "Hmm. I've always had a thing about pirates."

"*Arrrgggghhh*, pretty lady. Would you like to walk my plank?"

She erupted in giggles.

"Is it long enough to sit on?"

"Yes, definitely."

"Is it strong enough to hold my weight?"

"There's only one way to find out."

Still laughing, she spun herself around in the water until her arms settled around his neck and her legs straddled his waist. She felt something deep inside her roar with hunger when she sensed his penis pulsing against her entrance.

"God, Nick. I don't know what it is about you, but all I can think of when you're around is getting down and dirty with you."

"Good. Then you won't mind if I do this…" he said, moving his hand over her until one finger found the hardening bunch of nerves at her center.

"Not at all."

"And if I do this…?" he asked, gently flicking his finger back and forth.

Her brain short-circuited, leaving her unable to think of the right thing to say, so she just nodded.

"And what if I said I wanted all of you?"

The waves of pleasure he was creating with his finger melded with the cool lick of the surf passing back and forth across her, driving her crazy with need. Unable to speak, she shifted until he was almost inside her.

"Take me," she whispered. She knew she was being even more impulsive than usual, but she needed to know she was still alive and strong.

"It's safe?"

"Yeah. I'm on the Pill."

Growling wordlessly, he grabbed her butt in both hands and slammed all the way into her. She threw her head back and gave herself to his rhythm, rejoicing in the sensations his movement stirred up. Surely a body that could feel all this wasn't dying? She trembled on the precipice for longer than she would have thought possible, gasping and hungering for more of his touch. Then, with one final twist of his hips and a flick of his thumb, he sent her tumbling over the cliff.

She screamed with pleasure, her cries disappearing into the roar of the surf.

Seconds later he followed her over the edge. For a few

long moments afterward they clung to each other, swaying with the tide. Eventually she unlocked her legs from around his waist and let go, forcing her own feet to hold her weight.

She looked down at the water and for a moment couldn't believe her eyes.

"Nick? Is the water glowing?"

His eyes snapped open, then widened with wonder. "It certainly is."

As far as the eye could see the water sparkled with tiny green dots of phosphorescence. The lights fluttered and swirled in the waves, almost seeming to move to a choreographed dance.

Her heart thrilled. Maybe her mom really was trying to talk to her. "The fairies followed us, Nick."

"Either that or we attracted a whole new batch."

She smiled and leaned back against him, letting her feet float in front of her. "I could stay out here forever."

"Not me. My fingers are turning into prunes."

"Was that a manly way of asking if we could go back to shore, or something?"

"Or something."

She giggled and grabbed his hand. "Let's go, then."

Hand in hand, they splashed through the water back to dry land, the wet sand sucking at their toes. When they reached their clothes she rose up on her tiptoes and kissed him. "Thank you for coming with me, Nick."

"Thank you for inviting me. This place really is paradise."

"*Ouch.* That hurts. What the hell…?"

Jessie looked down and saw that a little yellow crab was pinching her with everything he had.

"Peace, little guy," she said, trying to shake him off. But he wouldn't let go.

Finally Nick reached down and pried his claws off. The

crab skittered off and Jessie sat down in the sand to check her toe, which was red and bleeding.

"*Damn*, that hurts," Jessie hissed.

"You probably shouldn't walk on that. Let me carry you."

Suddenly exhausted, Jessie decided not to argue. Instead, she just held out her arms. He scooped her up and kissed her forehead.

"I guess even paradise has its monsters."

"Yes, it does But they're a whole lot easier to deal with when you're not alone," she mumbled sleepily.

"Jessie?"

"Hmm?"

"How do we get in the house?"

"There's a keypad. The code is 530178. The bedroom is right at the top of the stairs."

"All right. I got you, princess. You can relax now."

Feeling safer than she had since her mom died, Jessie snuggled deeper into his arms and let herself fall asleep.

The smell of pancakes and frying meat filled the air. Nick yawned and stretched, feeling marvelously relaxed. He couldn't remember the last time he'd slept as well as he had last night.

Deciding to skip a shower, he dragged a pair of swim trunks out of the duffel bag Bob had packed for him and headed out to the kitchen—only to stop dead.

Jessie twirled and shimmied her way around the bright red room, dancing to the beat of whatever music was piping through her earbuds. Her neon green string bikini shifted as she swayed, each corner of the bottom slowly creeping up over her softly rounded butt until it seemed the fabric would meet in the middle. She grabbed the spatula she was using to flip the pancakes and held it to her mouth.

"Searching the world for a hero," she belted out, throwing her head back like a pop star. "Hoping he can save me from myself. Yeah, I'm searching for my hero…"

Nick grinned and padded over to where she stood. When she didn't seem to see him, he tapped her on the shoulder.

She shrieked, jumping straight into the air. When she saw it was him she pulled the headphones from her ears.

"Where did you come from?"

"I'm from the hero home delivery service. You call—we answer. Twenty-four hours a day."

She blinked, then grinned. "Wow, that was fast. Okay, hero, can you grab some plates for me, please? They're in that cupboard over there."

Nick got some blue flowered plates down and set them on the counter.

"My hero," she said, before piling a stack of pancakes and thick slices of bacon on each plate. "Let's go eat these in the lanai."

Nick opened the sliding door that separated the screened-in deck from the kitchen.

"Ladies first."

She breezed past him and sat, a wide smile spreading across her face as she took in the view. "Better than New York in March, huh?"

"Definitely," he said, pausing to appreciate the gorgeous turquoise water and sun-kissed sand that lay below them. But he couldn't stop thinking about her singing. "What did you want to do when you were a kid?"

"Cause trouble?"

"No, for a living? When you grew up?"

"Sing," she said without hesitation. "I wanted to be on Broadway."

He nodded, not surprised. "I thought so. Every time I turn around you're singing and dancing. Why didn't you?"

"Become a singer?"

He nodded again.

She shrugged. "I just realized I wasn't talented enough, I guess."

"I don't believe that for a second."

She raised her eyebrow. "And why not?"

He blinked. It seemed so obvious. How could she not see it?

"You were made for the stage, Jessie. You're gorgeous, you're vibrant…everything about you is bigger than life. And your voice is spectacular."

"You're a talent agent now?"

"No, but I've cast enough commercials to know talent when I see it."

And he knew more than a few talent agents who would pay dearly to have someone like her on their roster.

"Life just didn't work out that way," she said, then stuffed her mouth full of pancake.

Clearly, it wasn't a topic she cared to discuss.

She ate in silence for a few minutes, long enough for Nick to start to worry that he'd seriously annoyed her. He racked his brain, trying to think of something to say that would make it better, but came up blank. Redheads certainly were volatile creatures.

"I just don't talk about it," she said finally.

"You don't have to. I shouldn't have said anything."

"No, it's okay. I want to tell you." She reached over and squeezed his hand. "It's a good weekend to vanquish ghosts."

He wasn't sure how to respond to that, so he stayed quiet.

She looked down at her plate, playing with her fork while she talked. "I was serious about my singing. Went to voice lessons and the whole ball of wax. The summer I was sixteen I won a part in a regional tour of *The Sound of Music*. I was going to be Liesl. I was over the moon—my parents even agreed to let me travel by myself. But then, three weeks before we were supposed to leave, my mom got her cancer diagnosis. They said she only had eight weeks to live. I dropped out, of course, and she died six weeks later."

He tried to imagine what that must have been like, but couldn't. "Oh, my God, Jessie. I didn't realize it was so sudden."

She grimaced. "Yeah. It was awful. After she died my dad shut down. It was up to me to take care of Gloria and keep the house running. Looking back, I can see that he was depressed—but at the time I just thought he was being a jerk."

"Understandably so."

She nodded. "Yeah. Anyway, I kept that up for about six months. Just when I was at the end of my rope my choir teacher suggested I audition for Julliard's summer program. I did…and I got in. But when I told my dad he was furious."

Her face crumpled, and Nick could see she was fighting back tears.

"He told me I couldn't go—and that I was terribly selfish for even wanting to. He said I had to stay and take care of my sister. I was livid. And I told him… I told him that I hated him. And that he was so useless as a father we'd be better off without him."

She stopped and took a deep breath.

"That night he had a heart attack and died. I found him the next morning."

For the first time since she started her story, she looked at him and the anguish in her eyes was almost unbearable.

"I blamed myself, of course. I gave up singing as a kind of penance. I didn't mean for it to be forever, but then I found a second love in advertising and here we are, fourteen years later. Life happens, you know?"

He got up and knelt down in front of her chair. "You know it wasn't your fault, right?"

She nodded, tears still leaking down her face.

"I'm sure your dad wouldn't have wanted you to blame yourself."

"No, he wouldn't have."

"Will you let me hold you?"

She nodded again and crawled into his lap, burying her head against his chest. He stroked her hair gently as her hot tears tracked down his stomach. A wave of overwhelming tenderness swamped him. Try though he might, he couldn't deny that this woman was something special. He knew he'd do anything to keep her from getting hurt again—even if it meant he had to give up on the Goddess account. He'd find another way to save Thornton.

She pulled back a little so she could wipe her tears and gave him a watery smile.

"I've been an excellent weekend date so far, haven't I? This is the second time I've cried on you. I'll bet you're ready to go home."

"Not at all. I'm happy you feel safe enough to talk with me. But," he said, getting to his feet while still holding her, "I think you've shed enough tears in Paradise. Fortunately, I happen to have a foolproof way to distract you."

"And what would that be?"

"I'll have to take you into the bedroom to show you."

"Then what are you waiting for? To the bedroom!"

Nick set her down on the red hibiscus-printed comforter and straddled her hips. "You look like some sort of exotic tropical bird lying there."

"And you look a hawk, ready to swoop down and eat me up."

His eyes glittered. "In that case I'll start by pecking off this bikini top."

His hands reached for the tie at the back of her neck.

She slapped his hands away. "No!"

He backed off, looking wounded. "What's wrong?"

Jessie sighed. How could she explain without telling him about the biopsy?

"I fell yesterday and managed to bang up my right side. My breast is pretty bruised today."

He raised an eyebrow. "And how did you do that?"

Good question. "Well, my sister was doing laundry and didn't realize she'd left a bra lying in the middle of the hallway. I slipped on it and, well…down I went. I landed on a stiletto."

There. That sounded plausible—didn't it?

"Huh." He didn't look as if he believed her. "So what you're saying is I should be very careful with your breasts today?"

"Or you could just leave them alone entirely."

That seemed like the better option to her. The less he touched them, the less she would be reminded of what might be lurking inside.

"Nah. I think I'd rather kiss it better."

Once again, Nick reached for her halter tie.

"Nick…"

He put a finger on her lips. "Shush. Trust me. I know what you need to feel better."

She really didn't want him to look at the rainbow-hued mess that was her right breast. "But, Nick…"

Nick gently grabbed her arms. "Do I have to tie you up to get you to accept your medicine?"

Her blood buzzed at the thought. "No, that won't be necessary. I just…"

He shook his head at her and pulled her hands over her head. "Grab the headboard."

"What? Why?"

"Just do it."

Her heart beat wildly in her chest. She was torn between panic and extreme desire. She wasn't used to being so submissive. Wasn't sure she *could* give up control so completely.

"Keep them there or I really will tie you up."

She nodded silently, not trusting herself to speak.

Slowly, surely, Nick untied her bikini top. She tensed, ready for him to say something unflattering. But he didn't.

"Poor baby, you really did get beat up. It's going to take some time to kiss this all better."

He settled down on top of her, resting his weight on his arms, and began kissing a slow circuit around her breast. She tensed when he reached the bandage covering the needle marks, but his lips skated across it as if it was just another piece of her skin.

When he grazed the sensitive skin of her aureole, her hands started to drift down of her own accord. He stopped her with a look. "Do I need to go find some rope?"

She hastily grabbed the headboard again.

"Good girl."

Jessie closed her eyes and willed herself to let go.

Nick worshipped each breast equally, circling them with his kisses and sucking her nipples. She began to relax as her body tuned into what was being done to it and had the predictable reaction.

Heat exploded in her breasts, sending delicious sensations spiraling into every part of her and she whimpered.

"Oh, you like that, do you? I told you you would." Nick looked up at her, his eyes glinting with desire. "Tell me what you want next."

She shook her head. Now that she had let him have control, she didn't want to take it back.

"Oh, so *that's* how you want to play it?" Nick took one hand and slid it between her wet folds. "I guess I'll have to do things my way, then."

She nodded again.

He dived, and soon his fingers had been replaced by his tongue. He licked and nibbled and sucked in a random pattern that kept her from finding a satisfying rhythm. Need swelled until it became almost painful.

She grabbed Nick's head. "Nick—please!"

He stopped and looked up at her. "What did I say about those hands?"

Slowly she reached up to grab the headboard again.

"Oh, that was much too slow. Just for that I'm not going to let you come this way."

She couldn't stop the growl that rose through her throat. She didn't think she could stand it any longer.

"Oh, don't worry. You'll still get there. It's just going to take a little longer.

He rose up and thrust into her, all in one movement. She gasped as she adjusted to the feeling of fullness.

"Oh, you feel perfect. Don't move." He pinned her wrists with one big hand and smiled down at her.

"I won't," she managed to say.

"Good girl."

He slammed into her again and again, until she felt the orgasm sparkling at the corners of her eyes.

He saw her body arching and smiled. "Come for me, baby."

That was one request she was happy to oblige. She felt the fireworks explode in her veins. Seconds later she heard him yell as his release found him.

When they had both stopped panting he kissed her, long and slow. "It's a good thing we both know this is temporary," he said.

"Why?"

"Because sex like that could quickly become addictive."

She laughed, but said nothing. She had a bad feeling she might already be hooked.

* * *

The sun was much higher in the sky the next time Jessie got out of bed.

"How do you feel about snorkeling?" she asked as she grabbed her bikini bottom from where it had landed on the ceiling fan.

"Fine, I guess…" Nick answered, frowning as he looked at his phone.

"Would you like to go? All the equipment's here, and there's an excellent reef not too terribly far away."

"Sure. But I need to call my father first. Apparently there's some sort of crisis there."

She nodded. "Got it. I'll just be out in the kitchen, getting a cooler together."

He grunted, already punching the number into his phone.

She puttered about in the kitchen, stashing a couple of bottles of beer, some sandwich stuff, and a container of chocolate cookies she found on the counter in the cooler. Then she gathered up beach towels and retrieved the snorkeling equipment from the closet on the ground floor and took it all down to the golf cart.

When he still hadn't appeared by the time she'd finished, she decided to check and see if he'd changed his mind. If he had, she'd just go by herself. She padded through the house in her bare feet and was about to knock on the bedroom door when she heard Nick yelling.

"Dad, I'm doing the best I can! You have to give me some time. We'll have more work than we know what to do with by the end of the year."

His father's voice crackled through the speaker on Nick's cell phone. "Well, Media Incorporated isn't going to leave their offer on the table forever. The shareholders are asking me for a decision by the end of the month."

Nick sighed. "Please say no. We don't need their money."

"I wish I could trust you, Nick. But you don't seem very dedicated. I'm here in the office right now. Where are *you*?"

"I had to leave town for the weekend."

"Great. Just great. Meanwhile, that lion woman of yours is running around the city stealing all of our clients."

"No, she's not. Trust me on that one."

"How do you know? Unless she's there with you. I told you I didn't want you seeing her."

Nick didn't say anything.

"She is, isn't she? Listen, Nick. If you want me to turn down this offer I'm going to need to see more loyalty from you. Give her a good screw this weekend, then forget about her."

"And if I don't?"

"Then I'll sell the agency and move to Boca before the month is out. *I* don't care what happens to this place. You're the one that's all worried about upholding a dead man's wishes."

"You're a bastard."

"Damn straight. I expect to see you here bright and early Monday morning, ready to screw Roar over—not screw Roar's owner."

Nick growled and hung up.

Jessie scurried away from the door, hoping he wouldn't realize that she'd heard every word.

She was pouring a glass of water from the sink by the time he emerged from the bedroom.

"Ready?" she asked with forced enthusiasm, her back to him.

"Sure am!"

She heard the same note of falseness in his voice.

"Great. Everything's already in the golf cart."

"Cool."

A painful awkwardness hung in the air for the entire two-mile drive. The longer the silence held, the angrier she got. Was he just going to pretend that everything was fine? Was he wishing he could get in the car and leave now? And, if that was the case, why didn't he? She didn't need him to enjoy this place. In fact, it would probably be better without him.

When they got to the snorkeling cove she slammed the golf cart into "park" and stomped away into the sand. Why didn't he *say* something? Was he just going to sit like a lump until their plane left tomorrow?

"Jessie?" said a cautious voice behind her.

"What?"

"What's wrong?"

Jessie turned to glare at him. "What's *wrong*? What's *not* wrong? I heard you talking to your father. I heard him tell you to screw me, then screw me over. And I *didn't* hear you refuse to do so. So what am I supposed to do? Snuggle up to you and pretend nothing's wrong? Take you into my bed, knowing you're going to try and put me out of business on Monday? What do you want me to do?"

"Nothing."

"Nothing? You want me to do *nothing*?" Her body burned with anger. She wanted to hit him, or kick him, or… or… She picked up a handful of sand and threw it at him.

"Take that!" she shouted, and reached down to grab another handful, which she threw at him with all her might. "And that!"

Unfortunately the sand was dry, so her weapon dissipated into a cloud of dust before it ever reached him.

"Arrrggghhh!" she shrieked, too angry to form words.

Nick smiled at her. "You're doing it wrong."

"What?"

"You're doing it wrong. If you want to pelt me with sand you need to go where the sand is wet, so you can mold it like a snowball. Here—let me show you."

He ran down to the wet sand at the water's edge and patted a ball of sand together in his hands. Then he wound his arm up in classic pitcher's style and lobbed it at her.

It hit her square in the face before she had time to duck. For a moment she stood stock-still, too shocked to move. Then the rage returned, and before she realized what she was doing she was running down the beach at him, shrieking incoherently. As she approached she tucked her head down and aimed for his chest—just as the high school football player she had once dated had taught her.

She barreled into him and they both went down in a tangle of arms and legs. "I hate you, I hate you, I *hate you!*" she shouted, pummeling his chest with her fists.

"No, you don't."

"What did you say?"

"I said, no. You don't."

The sheer audacity of the statement stopped her cold. How could he say that? Didn't he know what he'd done to her? She was still goggling at him when he grabbed her hands and neatly flipped her over, pinning her in the sand.

"You don't hate me. And you shouldn't. I have no intention of 'screwing you over,' as my father suggested. He is a clueless old man who insists on believing he still knows what's what. But he doesn't. And I don't listen to him."

"Why should I believe you?"

He grinned. "Because if I was going to screw you over you would feel it when I did this."

Keeping her hands pinned, he claimed her lips for his own with a kiss that demanded she respond. For a moment she resisted. Refused to give him what he wanted. But he kept nibbling, and sucking, and demanding she give in.

Desire rushed through her lips and infected every part of her body until every single skin cell vibrated with want. Hating herself for doing so, she opened her mouth, letting his tongue invade. His appreciation rumbled through her chest and something primitive inside her roared to life. Her anger mixed with want, creating an explosive ball of need.

She wrapped her legs around him, wordlessly showing him what she wanted, but when her hips rose up against his he just chuckled. Moments later, he broke off the kiss.

"What are you *doing*?" she sputtered.

"Keeping you from doing something you might regret."

"I won't." Her legs locked even tighter around him.

"You will. This is a public beach and it's one o'clock in the afternoon. I don't want to have to call my father to bail us out of jail."

He had a point.

Reluctantly, she unlaced her feet, letting her legs sprawl loosely in the sand. "Fine. Let go of me."

"Not until you admit you don't hate me."

"I don't hate you. I just hate the situation we're in."

He sat up and stretched, then looked down at her with a grimace on his face. "I hate it too. I wish we could just enjoy each other."

Jessie's lips turned down. "Don't."

"Don't what?"

She sat up and dusted the sand off her arms. She needed to stop that line of thinking cold. "Don't start wishing. Let's just enjoy the time we have. It's not like either of us is interested in anything long-term anyway. It's just for the weekend, right?"

He stared at her for a moment and then nodded his assent. "All right. What time does our flight leave tomorrow?"

"Four-thirty, I think. Why?"

"From now until four-thirty tomorrow neither one of us is allowed to mention Roar, Thornton, New York City, or even advertising. We are just two ordinary people, frolicking on the beach."

She snorted. "I don't think I've ever heard anyone use the word 'frolicking' outside of advertising."

"Well, whatever you want to call it. We are here—at the beach. I'm just an ordinary guy who thinks you're fantastic, and you're just a smart babe who has deigned to come away with me for the weekend. No one and nothing else matters. Deal?"

She stuck her hand out. "Deal."

"Great. Then let's go snorkeling."

They stayed out in the surf for hours, admiring the multi-colored fish, chasing crabs, and once even petting a sting-ray. When at long last the sun began to set, they splashed out of the water hand in hand.

Nick's stomach growled. "What were you thinking of for dinner?"

Jessie grinned. "I've got a treat in store for you."

"Uh-oh. What kind of treat? Do I have to catch my dinner with a paper clip and some silly string?"

"Nope. But you might have to pay for it with a power ballad or two."

He groaned. "I think I'd rather try the silly string."

"Don't be a wuss," she said, throwing a T-shirt at him from the back of the golf cart.

"I'm not. Just being realistic."

"You say realistic—I say wusstastic."

"Say that when I can reach you," he said, grabbing at her bikini top.

She giggled and danced to the other side of the golf cart, sliding into the driver's seat. "Keep your hands to yourself and get in the cart. The dinner bus is leaving."

"All right, all right," he fake grumbled as he climbed in. "But trust me when I tell you no one wants to hear me sing."

"We'll see," she said, and put the cart into gear.

A few minutes later they rolled into what passed for a

parking lot—a patch of bare sand where golf carts could congregate. There was no restaurant as he understood the term. Just a tiki hut that seemed to house the kitchen, a bunch of people seated at brightly colored picnic tables, and palm trees covered in fairy lights. A makeshift stage stood at one end of the beach, although at the moment a boom box on the tiki hut's front counter provided the only source of music.

A large white-haired woman wearing a pink and lime-green flamingo print maxi-dress came barreling toward them.

"Jessie! You're here!"

Jessie's eyes opened wide. "*Mama Dora?* But I haven't seen you in fifteen years!"

The woman swallowed Jessie up in a bear hug. "I know—and that's thirteen years too many! Mimi told me you were coming." She stepped back and looked Jessie over with a critical eye. "You, my dear, need to eat. Bellies aren't supposed to be concave!"

"I know. I've just been under a lot of stress."

"Well, now you're with Mama Dora. And I'm going to fatten you up."

She was about to lead Jessie away when she noticed Nick standing there.

"Is this your young man?"

"Just for the weekend." Jessie winked at Mama.

She raised an eyebrow. "Welcome, welcome, Jessie's young man for the weekend."

He grinned. "It's Nick. And thank you."

"All right—no need to stand on ceremony. Let's get you two seated so I can get some food into this girl." She put one arm around both of them and led them to a lime-green picnic table under a palm tree. "Any food allergies I should know about?"

They both shook their heads.

"Good, good. Dinner will be out shortly."

She swept away as quickly as she had come. Nick raised an eyebrow at Jessie. "Don't we get a menu?"

"Nope. At Mama's you just eat what she gives you. But don't worry. It's always excellent."

Seconds later she was back. This time armed with a trash can lid full of food. "Here we are. Pulled pork, fresh conch, jicama slaw, and a pitcher of mango mamaritas."

"Mamaritas?" Jessie asked.

"They're like margaritas, but better. Eat up! Karaoke begins soon."

Nick swallowed. "There really is karaoke, huh?"

Jessie laughed. "You bet. And dancing."

"Oh, boy. Forget eating up. I better drink up."

"Me too."

They ate in companionable silence, watching the other diners whoop it up. It was a colorful crowd, an even mix of senior citizens, honeymooners, and young families. They all had only one thing in common—they were having fun.

"When I grow up this is what I want to do, I think," Jessie said.

"What? Eat?"

"No. Own a place like this. Not necessarily on a beach, but a bar or a restaurant, or something, where the only requirement is to have fun. I'll have karaoke every night and take the stage whenever I want to. Wouldn't that be amazing?"

He smiled at her. "I'm not sure if *amazing* is the word, but it does seem like something that would make you happy."

She nodded. "Actually, I've often thought about buying the Happy Hour."

"What's that?"

"The eighties club I took you to. Those are *my* people."

He remembered the way they had applauded for her. She'd been in her element there.

"So why don't you?"

"Why don't I what?"

"Buy it."

She gave him a funny smile, pausing to finish her mamarita before answering. "My capital is currently all tied up in a little thing called Roar. As is my time."

"Well, if you would let me buy Roar…"

She held up her hand. "Stop right there. We are *not* having this conversation right now."

He tried to think of something to say to that, but was spared by the screech of microphone feedback.

"Whoops—sorry about that, folks!" Mama said. "But now that I've got your attention I'd like to invite a very special guest on stage. I haven't seen her in more than a decade, but I'm guessing she still knows the words to this song."

Jessie squealed as the introductory chords played. "That's my song!"

"I know it is, dear. Now, get up here!" Mama said through the microphone.

Jessie sprang up from her chair and danced toward the stage. Nick breathed a sigh of relief, thinking he was off the hook.

But at the last minute she beckoned to him. "Come on, Nick. You know this one."

He tried shaking his head, but the other restaurant patrons hooted and hollered, urging him on. Reluctantly, he made his way toward Jessie.

"I'm warning you: I'm no good at this."

"Nobody cares," she said.

Then the music started and Jessie launched into the song, crooning about rainbows and love. The fairy lights lit a halo around her fiery hair, making her glow with an ethereal beauty. When she smiled at him all the breath left his body as an epiphany hit him in the gut. At some point in the last twenty-four hours, he had fallen completely and hopelessly in love with this woman. This completely inappropriate, crazy, wonderful woman.

Damn.

Two hours later he found himself sitting on the beach alone, hoping to find an answer to his dilemma in the slate-gray depths of the waves. He was adamantly opposed to relationships. Had never imagined himself entering into anything long-term.

But the thought of Jessie with someone—anyone else—made him want to punch something. Hard. He wanted her for himself. Forever. But could he do it? He let himself imagine their lives together. Working side by side, riding home on his Harley, making love…everywhere.

The thought didn't scare him. So he took it one step further. Pictured a baby in Jessie's arms. A red-haired baby, of course. And found himself smiling.

Whoa.

All right. So obviously, his psyche was willing to give this relationship thing a shot. And when he thought about it the business side of him agreed. What better way to get rid of the Goddess problem than to tie the proprietress of Roar to him—and to Thornton by extension?

The problem would be getting *her* to agree. She'd made it very clear that she didn't do relationships.

He jumped when a bottle of wine was thunked into the sand next to him.

"You were right," Jessie said as she sat down.

Nick took a deep breath to calm himself. "Right about what?"

She reached for the wine bottle and began pouring it into the two insulated wine tumblers she'd brought with her. "You can't sing."

He laughed. "Told you so."

She grinned back at him. "It was very gallant of you to do it anyway."

"It seems I'd do just about anything for you. First skinny-dipping, then singing in public—all within twenty-four hours! You should feel special."

He said it with a smile, but in his heart he knew it was no joke.

"I do." She squeezed his hand.

"Do what?"

"Feel special. You've been amazing this weekend. I want you to know I really appreciate it. If only…"

"If only what?" His senses were on high alert. Did she have feelings for him? God, he hoped so.

"Never mind. I said we weren't allowed to play the 'what if?' game this weekend."

"Go ahead. I want to hear what you were going to say."

She stared off into space, seeming to search the stars for answers. "I just wish things were different. That I'd met you in a different life or something—you know?"

Nick was silent for a long moment as he argued with himself. Logically, he knew he should leave it at that. But he couldn't.

"I know. But, Jessie, we don't have to give up on this. I know it will be complicated, but we can make it work."

She shook her head sharply from side to side. "No. I don't do relationships. Period."

Nick felt himself growing frustrated, even though he had known that was what she'd say.

"Jessie, do you have feelings for me?"

She glared at him. "I won't allow myself to have feelings for you."

He brushed the hair off her forehead. "Well, pretend you did allow yourself."

Her mouth pulled back in a snarl and she stood up, angrily brushing sand off her butt.

"If you really must know—then, yes. You're the first man I've ever met that I can imagine having a future with. But I don't want to feel that way. I don't *want* to have a future with anybody. I. Don't. Do. Love."

She turned and stalked away, but not before Nick saw the angry tears in her eyes.

He went after her, determined to make her listen.

"Jessie!" he called as he paced after her.

She crossed her arms around her chest and sped up.

He broke into a run, circling in front of her. He was just going to have to lay it all out on the line and hope for the best. He took a deep breath.

"Jessie, I think I'm in love with you."

She stopped and stared at him. "What did you say?"

"Jessie, I think I love you."

Her face crumpled and she flew at him, fists flying. "How dare you say that to me? How *dare* you?" she screeched, tears flowing down her face. "That isn't fair!"

Nick grabbed her fists in his hands and pulled her to him as gently as he could. "I know it's too soon to say that to you. I don't expect you to feel the same way. But if you'll give me a chance—if you'll take a chance on us—I promise I'll find a way to make this work, Jessie. I *promise*."

"I c-c-can't," she said between tears. "You don't know what you're asking of me."

"Yes, I do. And I know you can. You just have to be brave. And you, Jessie, are the bravest woman I've ever met."

She took a shuddering breath and looked up at him, her eyes searching his in the moonlight.

"I don't feel very brave right now. I'm scared."

"Can you tell me why?"

"I really don't want to."

He let go of her fists and cupped her face with his hands. "Please try."

She shook her head. "I can't. Not yet. But I will soon."

"All right. That will have to be good enough," he said, trying not to let her see his frustration. "But can you at least agree to see where this takes us? If you decide tomorrow that you hate me and you never want to see me again I'll go. But if you don't I'd like to stay."

"I can't promise you forever, Nick."

"I'm not asking for forever. I'm just asking for tomorrow."

She shook her head.

"Please?" He let his expression show her how much her answer meant to him.

She growled. "Goddamn it, Nick."

He didn't respond. He knew silence was his best weapon right now.

She paced a little way down the beach and kicked at the surf again and again. He smiled when he heard a litany of expletives hit the air. She was coming around.

Finally she stalked back to him. When they were standing almost nose to nose, she spoke. "Fine. You can have tomorrow. But, Nick, if you try and use my emotions against me—if you try to take Roar from me…"

"I won't." He wouldn't.

"And don't expect me to get all girlfriendy. I don't even know how to *be* a girlfriend."

"I never would." He didn't know how to be a boyfriend either.

"Then fine. One day at a time."

"Thank you."

She tilted her lips up to his, wordlessly asking him to kiss her. He did as she asked, intending to keep it soft and gentle. The moment his lips touched hers, though, she melted against him, seeming to want to absorb him into her skin.

He let his lips and tongue communicate the wild heat that sizzled in his veins, lashing and sucking and claiming her mouth for his own. He slid his hands down her body, undoing the strings of her bikini one by one, desperate to remove all the physical barriers between them. Finally she was bare in front of him.

"You are amazing," he whispered, then kissed a burning path down her neck, past her shoulder and around her breasts, imprinting the feel of them on his mouth.

She whimpered and pulled on his swim trunks.

"Not yet," he said, laying her back on the sand.

He wanted to claim every part of her for his own. Spreading her legs, he kissed his way up to her warm, hot center. Gently he nibbled at her sensitive folds, loving the way she tasted. Wanting more, he dove in to suck and tease. In no time at all her legs wrapped themselves around his head and he lost himself in her intoxicating scent as she came against his mouth.

"That's my girl," he said, then moved up her body, worshiping every inch of her with his kisses.

When he came close enough she grabbed at his shirt, sliding it over his head. He let her, then slid his swim trunks off.

"In. Now," she said.

He did as she asked, groaning when she closed around him. He'd never met a woman who fit him so perfectly, so deliciously. It was as if she was made for him.

Jessie smiled up at him and bucked her hips. "What are you waiting for?"

He grinned. "I thought I'd just hang out for a while and enjoy the view."

"Didn't you see the 'No Loitering' sign? If you want me to keep you around, you've got to work harder than that."

He laughed and twisted his hips to bump against her sensitive spots. "How's that?"

She gasped. "That's more like it."

He began moving slowly, enjoying the play of emotions on her face as she gave herself over to desire. Eventually, though, she grew restless and her hips came up to meet his.

"Still. Not. Working. Hard. Enough," she gasped.

He laughed. "Impatient, are we?"

She nodded.

"As you wish, my love."

He slammed into her, fast and hard, the fire in his own body burning ever hotter as she got closer and closer to the edge. Finally her head dropped back and she gave herself to her orgasm, screaming his name. When her muscles clenched around him his own orgasm roared through him, made stronger by the love that bubbled in his veins.

For better or worse, she was his. He just had to prove to her it was for better.

CHAPTER NINE

THEIR REMAINING HOURS passed quickly, and almost before she could believe it was possible Jessie found herself seated in first class, watching the island she loved so much drop out of sight as the airplane climbed above the clouds.

She sighed, silently promising herself to visit Paradise again soon.

Nick squeezed her hand and smiled. "Aren't you glad I upgraded us?"

As the flight attendant came by with heated towels and cold champagne Jessie had to admit it was nice. "It's definitely a fitting end to a wonderful trip."

"The first trip of many."

"Maybe," she answered.

Nick frowned at her, but stayed silent.

She thought about apologizing, but despite what they'd said last night she wasn't sure where their relationship was going—or even if they would have one. She knew she had feelings for him. Big feelings that she had no idea how to process. But she also knew that there were big obstacles in their way.

Cancer. She might have it. Might be dying of it. And if that was the case...

She pictured Nick driving her to doctor's appointments and caring for her when chemotherapy made her too weak to do it herself. The thought soothed her. It would be nice not to have to go through that alone.

Unbidden, an image of her father from the months after

her mother's death appeared in her mind. Stooped. Gray. Lifeless.

She could never put Nick through that.

Not for the first time she sent a prayer winging…somewhere. Maybe to her mother's ears. She'd give anything to have the biopsy come out negative.

Nick reached over to squeeze her knee. "Penny for your thoughts?"

He'd have to pay a lot more than that before she told him what she was thinking.

"Oh, I was just trying to figure out a game plan. For when we get home. I have a lot of work to do."

"Does your game plan include me?"

The squint around his eyes gave away how tense he was about the subject.

"Sure."

His shoulders visibly relaxed as she watched. Time to turn the tables.

"What's *your* game plan? How are you going to get your dad off my back?"

He gave her a long, slow smile. "Well, you could still sell Roar to me. That would do the trick."

Her mouth dropped open. Surely he wasn't serious. "You *are* kidding, right?"

He grinned. "Mostly. Although it would be nice."

She glared at him.

He sighed. "Don't worry, I have other ideas. I've got to make some phone calls before I can tell you about them, though."

Jessie took a deep breath. There was something she needed to know if there was going to be any hope for them. "Nick?"

"Hmm?"

"Why are you so determined to stick with Thornton

& Co.? You have an amazing reputation. If you cut your losses and went out on your own you'd make a killing."

He scowled. "I have to."

That was *so* not an answer. "Why?"

He looked at her and sighed. "I promised my grandpa, okay? He never wanted my father to run it. Knew he didn't have what it takes to manage an agency of that size. So he made me swear that I'd take over for him at the earliest possible opportunity—and that I wouldn't let him destroy it."

Jessie blinked. "And is he? Destroying it?"

"Well, he sold shares in it to investors. And they want to sell it to some giant conglomerate. So...yes. And I'd never forgive myself if that happened."

Jessie squeezed his hand. "Damn, I wish I had asked you that a long time ago. Everything makes a lot more sense now."

He smiled sadly. "Well, now you know."

That she did. And now she knew she had to find a way to help him. But she was too damn tired to think. She couldn't stop the yawn that cracked her jaw open.

Nick smiled. "Enough about business. You need to rest. Want to see another reason why first class is so great?"

She nodded.

"Watch."

He pushed a button and both their seats moved backward into a fully reclining position.

"This is almost as comfy as a bed!' she said.

"It sure is. And you can use me as your pillow."

She didn't need to be told twice. She scooted next to him and curled up against his chest.

He kissed the back of her head. "Sweet dreams."

She was asleep before she could answer.

Jessie slept for the entire flight. When she came to, the plane was already beginning its descent.

"Good morning, sleepyhead," Nick said.

She yawned and smiled. "Hi, yourself. I think that was the best nap I've ever had."

"You're welcome. Think I should consider a career as a professional pillow?"

"Nope. I'd like to keep you as my little secret. I don't like to share my pillows. Cooties, you know."

He nodded, a serious expression on his face. "Right. Pillow cooties can be very contagious."

"All electronic devices, including mobile phones, can now be turned on," the flight attendant's voice crackled over the intercom. "But please stay in your seats until the fasten seatbelt sign is turned off."

Nick sighed. "I guess we can't put off re-entering the real world any longer."

Jessie reached under her seat for her purse and her phone. "I guess not."

"Wait," Nick said as her finger hovered over the power button. She paused, and he planted a kiss full of tenderness and longing on her lips.

"What was that for?"

"To thank you for the wonderful weekend. You are an amazing woman, Jessie."

Her heart swelled. It had definitely been one she'd never forget. "Thank you for coming with me."

"You bet." His expression turned serious. "But, Jessie... I think we'd better go our separate ways after the plane lands. It'd be best if we kept things on the down-low until after I get things with my father straightened out."

Jessie's smile faded. They weren't even off the plane yet and he was already thinking about hiding their romance. That stung.

Not wanting him to see how upset she was, she smiled and nodded. "Sure."

He smiled gratefully. "Thanks."

As soon as the flight attendant opened the door she grabbed her bag and fled. Unfortunately Nick followed, so she pretended to be deeply entranced by her phone until they got to the baggage carousel. Not surprisingly Bob was waiting for them when they got there, Jessie's hot pink overnighter in his hand.

"Hi, Bob! I'll take that from you," she said, reaching for the suitcase handle.

"Won't you be traveling back into the city with us?"

"No, I think it would be best if I get there under my own power. I know Nick's dad is expecting him at the office, and I don't want to take you out of your way."

Bob looked at Nick, who nodded. "She's right."

Bob shrugged. "Suit yourself."

Jessie kept the smile plastered to her face as she turned to Nick. "Thank you for the lovely weekend!" She stuck out her hand for him to shake, hoping he would kiss her instead. But he pumped it up and down, a funny look on his face.

"I'll call you."

"Please do. *After* you get things figured out with your dad."

"I will. By Wednesday at the latest."

She nodded. "I'll look forward to hearing from you."

Then she strode off, not waiting to hear his reply. Better for him to think she didn't need him than for him to see how hurt she was.

With luck, by the time she saw him on Wednesday he'd have things under control and she…she wouldn't have a cancer diagnosis.

Please, let them have a little luck this week.

"You ready?" Gloria asked as the car stopped in front of the cinderblock building that housed her doctor's office.

"No."

"Well, are you going to get out? Because the meter's running."

Jessie looked at Gloria and blinked, not understanding what she meant. Bob didn't have a meter. Then she remembered where she was—in a cab. Not Nick's limo.

"Right. Of course."

Jessie opened the door and forced herself to move. Once she was out, she stood stock-still, not wanting to go another step closer to her own personal hall of doom.

Gloria squeezed her arm. "It's going to be okay. No matter what the doctor says, it's going to be okay. I'm here for you."

Jessie nodded. "I know."

"Good. Then let's go!"

"I can't," Jessie whispered.

"Yes, you can. Here, I'll help."

Gloria grabbed her arm and pulled, towing Jessie behind her as she headed for the glass doors. Jessie followed, eventually convincing her legs to move under their own steam, but still not letting go of Gloria's hand.

She held it until they reached the thirty-fifth floor, home to the New York Cancer Diagnosis and Therapy Center.

"Here we are." Gloria smiled, but her voice shook.

Jessie nodded. "Yep."

"We've got to go in. You need to know what the doctor has to say."

"I know."

Gloria huffed. "So let's go."

Jessie looked at her, feeling helpless. "My knees are locked. I can't move."

Gloria gave her a gentle shove and she was off and running—or at least moving. She walked stiffly through the big oak door, not bothering to smile when the receptionist greeted her. Although the waiting room was just as uncomfortable today as it had been last week she didn't mind. In fact, she would be happy to stay there forever if it meant she didn't have to find out what her doctor had to say.

"Jessica Owens?"

Crap. They didn't seem to be running behind today.

"Do you want me to come with you?" Gloria asked.

Jessie nodded silently. Hand in hand, they followed the nurse back to the doctor's office. The small woman was already seated behind her desk when they got there, looking serious and wan in her white coat.

"Jessie! Gloria! It's good to see you! Have a seat, ladies."

Jessie sat. "What did you find out, Dr. Davies?"

The doctor sighed. "Jessie, before I start, I want you to promise to hear me out before you react, okay?"

Her heart plummeted. "It's cancer, isn't it?"

Dr. Davies nodded. "It is. But—and this is important—it's in Stage One. It's a contained lump and it hasn't spread—it hasn't even reached your lymph nodes."

Tears burned at the back of her throat. "But it's cancer?" she whispered.

"Yes, but Jessie, listen to me. Stage One cancer has a one hundred percent survival rate. You're going to be fine."

Jessie tried to listen, but a crazy voice in her head was chanting. *"Cancer. Cancer. Cancer. You're going to die of cancer."*

Jessie saw Gloria looking at her. Saw the concern in her face. But she couldn't do anything to reassure her. Couldn't even move her lips.

Gloria took control of the conversation. "What are our options?"

"We'll need to do surgery. I'd recommend a lumpectomy, but that's up to Jessie to decide…"

Their voices faded into the background as Jessie's mind replayed the last weeks of her mother's life for her.

She relived the day she'd come home from the doctor's office with her diagnosis and broken down in her father's arms. Saw her being wheeled away into surgery, a brave smile on her face as she waved to her daughters. Watched as she pulled clumps of hair from her head, tears pouring down her face. Felt the unbearable waves of agony when her dad had turned to her from where he was curled up against her mother's too still, too skinny body and said, "She's gone."

"I don't want to die," she heard herself wail. "Please don't let me die!"

Gloria's arms were around her in an instant. "You're not dying, Jessie. You're going to be fine. It's all going to be fine."

"I don't believe you!" the crazy person who had control of her voice shrieked. "I have cancer! It's not fine!"

Voices murmured over her head. "I don't know what's wrong. I can't get through to her," Gloria was saying.

"Perhaps a mild sedative?" someone else said.

Suddenly the doctor was there. "Jessie. I'm going to give you a shot. Just something to help you calm down."

She felt a pinch, and then darkness reached up to cradle her.

When Jessie came to she was lying on a gurney in a bright white exam room. Gloria was sitting slumped in the room's one chair, head thrown back, eyes closed. Jessie's body felt sore, as if she'd been fighting with giants in her sleep. Her mouth was dry. So dry. Looking around, she saw a sink on the other side of the room, a short stack of paper cups at the ready.

She had to get one of those.

She tried to sit up, but her head spun. Groaning, she fell back against the pillow.

Gloria's eyes snapped open. "Jessie! You're up! How are you feeling?"

"Like I've been trampled by a pack of hungry lions.

I was going to get a drink, but apparently my body's not ready to move yet."

Gloria scrambled up out of her chair. "I'll get it for you."

A moment later Jessie heard water running, then Gloria was pushing a small cup into her hand. "Here. Drink this."

She propped herself up on one elbow and drank it. It eased down her throat, making her feel more alive with every swallow.

"What happened to me back there?"

"You don't remember?"

Jessie shook her head. "I remember I freaked out. I just don't know why. It was like some incoherent stranger took over my brain."

Gloria frowned. "Dr. Davies said the trauma probably just tripped something in your brain. Kind of like a panic attack."

"Oh."

"Are you better now?"

Jessie thought about it for a second. Tried on the words *cancer patient*. Nothing happened. Thankfully, the irrational fear seemed to have played itself out.

"Yeah. I think so. But I didn't hear a thing about my treatment options."

"Don't worry about it. Dr. Davies said we could talk about it in a couple days—when you're feeling better. The important thing to remember is that you're going to be okay."

"All right. You know what would make me feel better right now?"

"What?"

Nick, she thought to herself. "A hot fudge sundae," she said out loud.

"That's the sister I know and love," Gloria said. "Off to Rachel's we go! We can handle anything with hot fudge in our bellies."

* * *

"Nick! How wonderful to see you," said a white-haired man as Nick walked through the double doors into the wood-paneled office.

Nick grinned, glad to see the Santa Claus lookalike who had been his family's lawyer for as long as he could remember. "Thanks for fitting me in, Peter."

"Nonsense. I always have time for you, my boy. Please, have a seat!"

Once they were seated in the red leather chairs arranged in front of the lawyer's crackling fireplace, Peter got a serious expression on his face. "There. Now, why don't you tell me what can I help you with? Do you need to have a prenuptial agreement drawn up?"

Nick blanched. "No, not today, Peter. I have a question about Thornton & Co."

"Ah, I see." Peter laced his fingers on his protruding stomach. "What is it that you want to know?"

"Well, I know that according to the terms of my grandfather's will the CEO title automatically becomes mine at the age of forty. Is there any way to speed that process along?"

"Can I ask why you need to know? Last I heard, you were on track to take that title from your father in the very near future."

Nick sighed. "My father and I are having a disagreement about the path the company should take. He is threatening to sell it before I get anywhere close to forty."

Peter frowned. "I see. Well, in that case, there *is* one way."

Nick sat up straight. "Lay it on me."

"You have to get married."

"Married?"

"Yes. According to your grandfather's will, if you are legally married, on your thirty-fifth birthday you automatically become CEO of Thornton & Co."

His thirty-fifth birthday was in four short weeks. Nick jumped up from his chair. "Peter, you are amazing. Thank you so much for the information!"

"Does it help?"

"You have no idea how much. Thank you!"

He whipped out his phone as he strode out of the office and texted Jessie.

I have news. Dinner tonight?

Her answer appeared in seconds.

Sure. Want to come to my place?

Nick grinned to himself.

Sounds great. I'll bring the food.

I knew I liked you. Be here by seven.

Nick put his phone to sleep and whistled as he waited for the elevator. That gave him just enough time to get his hair cut and stop at the jewelry store before heading to Jessie's.

It was going to be a great night.

"What are you going to tell him?" Gloria asked from her perch on the counter bar stool.

"I don't know. I haven't decided yet." Jessie waved at the table in front of her. "How does this look?"

"Crystal, china, real silver…even a tablecloth? It looks like you're planning to propose to him."

Jessie laughed, surprised at the brittleness in her voice. "That would be something. *Would you, Nick Thornton, go through cancer therapy with me? Will you hold my hand*

and feed me soup? And promise not to laugh when I lose my hair?"

"You're making a joke of it, but I'll bet he'd say yes," Gloria said, hopping off her chair.

Jessie was saved from answering by the sound of the doorbell roaring.

"Whatever. Go let him in, would you? And let your-self out?"

"Fine. But don't dismiss him out of hand, okay? He could really be a help to you in the months ahead."

Jessie waved her away and then went into the kitchen to pour the wine.

She was just putting the glasses on the table when he found her.

"Hey, babe," he said, putting two heavy bags down on the counter. "I brought a feast."

"Wow. You sure did." She walked over and peeked in-side. "What have we got here?"

"Thai, Italian and Indian. I wasn't sure what you were in the mood for."

She reached up on tiptoes and kissed him. He really was the most considerate guy on the planet. "Thank you. Let's just set it up here like a buffet. Then we can take little bits of everything!"

A comfortable silence fell as they unboxed the food and grabbed their plates. Jessie piled her dish high, but knew there was no way she was going to be able to eat. Her stom-ach was far too knotted to force food into it.

Once they were seated she did her best to get some small talk going.

"How was work today?"

He shrugged. "All right. I found a great warehouse space for Thornton Digital. It'll take a few months to make it work for our purposes, but when it's done it will look spec-tacular."

"Where are you keeping my people in the meantime?"

He looked up, his expression startled. She must have sounded more hostile than she'd intended.

"They're sharing an office next to mine. It's pretty nice. They can even see Central Park if they crane their necks."

She tried to smile. "Great. Take good care of them, okay? They're important to me."

He looked at her sharply. "Jessie, what's wrong? You look exhausted."

Great. Apparently Goddess's magic under-eye concealer wasn't so magic. "Guess you just wore me out over the weekend!"

"I don't believe you. Is everything okay at Roar?"

She nodded. "Becky called in some favors and roped a couple of great freelancers in to work for me. Don't tell Coleen, but the stuff they're putting together is even better than what she had going!"

"Glad to hear it. But if that's not the problem then what is?"

She sighed. "Just worried about what the future holds." It wasn't a lie.

"About that… I have some good news."

"Oh?" At least one of them did.

"I was going to wait until after dinner to do this, but what the heck?" He wiped his mouth with his napkin, then moved out her chair so he could kneel in front of her. "Jessie, I've found a way for us to be together. A way to take Thornton away from my dad and keep Roar safe."

Jessie's heart started to beat faster when she saw the serious look in his eyes. Whatever he was about to say, it was big.

He reached into his front pocket and drew out a little blue box. "Jessica Owens, will you do me the honor of becoming my wife?"

"What?"

Surely she had misheard him. But when he opened the box she realized he was completely serious. Inside was a beautiful ring, its center diamond glistening inside a nest of blood-red rubies.

"Jessie, I want you to marry me."

Her mouth went dry. "Why?"

"I went to see my lawyer today, and he said that if I was married by my thirty-fifth birthday Thornton legally becomes mine."

"When's your birthday?"

"Next month. But Roar would be safe even before then. As my wife, you'll be a Thornton. So the minute we're married the Goddess account will be back in the control of Thornton & Co. and our problems will be solved!"

Jessie's brain stuttered. He wanted to marry her. But did he want to marry *her*? Or did he just want her business? Had this been his plan all along?

"So you want to marry me to get your hands on Thornton—and Roar."

"What? No! Jessie, I love you!"

Rage flared to life in her heart. Jessie embraced it and let the flames spread.

"How do I know that? Maybe this has all been a ploy. Maybe your father's even behind it! Get the girl to fall in love, get her business, and then get rid of her!"

"Jessie, that's insane."

"No. You…this…this is insane."

He knelt back, his face pale. "You don't really believe that, do you?"

She drew a deep breath, trying to ignore the pain in her chest as her heart broke in pieces. "I don't know. But I do know I'm not going to marry you for business reasons."

"That isn't what I want, Jessie. I want—"

"I don't care what you want!" She pushed her chair back and spun away from him. Tears pricked at the backs of her eyelids. Damn it, she would *not* cry in front of him. "I'm not going to marry you! Just get out of here, will you?"

"But, Jessie…"

"But nothing. I don't want you here anymore. I don't need someone so manipulative in my life. Get *out*!"

He stood and his face turned to stone.

"Fine. I'll go. Have a nice life, Jessie. I hope Roar makes you very happy."

She listened as his footsteps receded and the door slammed. Once she was sure she was alone she collapsed on to the floor and released the sobs that had been building. Because everything she had told him was a lie. She did need him. She did want him. She was pretty sure she even loved him. But she wouldn't be a pawn in his business machinations.

For a moment she wished her cancer diagnosis was terminal. At least that way there would be an end date to the giant mess that she called her life.

CHAPTER TEN

Dear Jessie

I know you don't want to talk to me, but please don't delete this email before you read it. I need to apologize for what happened the other night.

I know how much you love Roar. And how desperate you are to shut down my father's attempts to sabotage it. I thought if I appealed to the businesswoman in you you'd agree to my plan—even though I know you don't love me.

But it was just a ploy to get you to say yes. There was nothing I wanted more than to make you my bride and live with you as man and wife—till death do us part and all that other sappy junk.

I'm sorry, Jessie. I hope you can find it in your heart to forgive me. And, above all, I hope that someday you find someone you can love the way I loved you.

Yours forever
Nick

Jessie read Nick's email for the two-hundredth time, not bothering to wipe the tears from her cheeks. How had things gone so wrong, so quickly?

Before he had arrived that night she'd had a plan all worked out in her head. She needed to take time out to take care of her health. He needed some time to get the business and his father under control. So she'd been going to propose that they take a break and start for real a few months later.

It would have worked.

But instead he'd made that stupid proposal. And she'd told him she never wanted to see him again. That she hated him.

There was no going back from that. His email made that very clear. He'd put "loved"—in the past tense. In fact he'd probably already moved on. So now she had to slog through cancer treatment without anything to look forward to on the other side.

"How's it going, Jess?"

Jessie jumped at the sound of her sister's voice and quickly clicked out of her email.

"Oh, you know. Terrible."

Gloria plopped down in her office's guest chair. "Well, that's not what I thought you were going to say. What's going on?"

Jessie rubbed her eyes and pushed back from her desk. She didn't want to talk about Nick with her sister, so she decided to talk about work instead.

"I'm designing garbage."

"I'm sure it's not that bad. Let me see."

Jessie spun the computer monitor around so Gloria could look at the screen.

"Hmm…"

"See—I was right. It sucks."

Gloria sighed. "It doesn't suck. It just doesn't have your usual flair."

Jessie shrugged. "I know. I just can't make myself care."

Gloria stared at her. "Who are you and what have you done with my sister? I thought you loved this campaign."

Jessie got up from her desk and crossed to the bay window, currently blocked with blackout drapes. She threw them wide and bright sunshine flooded the room.

"I did. I do. But I'm spending what could be my last days on earth huddled over my computer in the dark—and for what? To score a few points for feminists in the misogynist world of advertising? No matter how great these ads are, no one will even remember them in a few months. No one will remember *me*!"

Not even Nick, she thought to herself.

Gloria crossed the room and took Jessie's hands in hers. "Jessie, you're not dying. In a few months you'll have put cancer behind you and you can spend the rest of your life making sure everyone knows what Roar is and who you are. You could be an advertising legend!"

Jessie looked at her sister, but she didn't see her. In her mind's eye she saw her mother, looking shrunken and pale, lying in the middle of her parents' big four-poster bed.

"Come here, Jessie," she'd said, patting the bed next to her.

Jessie had crawled up.

"Lie down next to me."

Jessie remembered how anxious she'd felt. How afraid she'd been that she'd hurt her mother. But she'd done as she'd asked, curling up next to her on the pillow.

When they'd been eye to eye, her mother had reached out and brushed the hair away from her face.

"Jessie, you know I'm dying, right?"

Jessie had nodded as tears began to leak down her cheeks.

Her had mom wiped them away. "Oh, no, baby, don't cry. Don't cry. You're going to be okay."

"How can you say that? You're leaving me."

"I know, honey. I know. But I'll still be watching over you. You won't be able to see me, but I'll be there."

She'd grabbed her mother's hand. "But, Mommy, I…"

Her mom had placed a finger on her lips. "Shh. Listen. Whenever you're missing me, and wishing I was there to help you, I want you to promise me you'll do something."

"What?"

"Stop. Listen to your heart. And ask yourself, *Will this,*

whatever it is I'm about to do, make me happy? And if it will you'll know you're doing what I would want you to do."

"I don't understand!"

Her mother had smiled. "All I want is for you to be happy. Do what brings you joy. And never forget: it's not the things you do, but the people you love that matter the most. Love is what makes life worth living…"

"Jessie? Jessie are you okay?"

Jessie blinked and the world came back into focus. "Gloria, I've been doing it wrong," she whispered.

Gloria frowned. "Doing what wrong? What are you talking about?"

"Life. I've been doing it wrong. Worrying too much about making my mark on the world and not enough about making memories with the people who matter."

Gloria tugged on her hand. "Jessie, I think you need to sit down. You're not making sense."

Jessie took a deep breath. "No. Wait. What I'm trying to say is that I've realized Roar doesn't matter that much in the big scheme of things. People are what matters, and I've spent too long keeping myself closed off. I'm tired of being afraid. Of refusing to take a chance on love. I've been pouring everything I have into Roar. I don't want it to be all that matters anymore."

Gloria stepped back. "Whoa. It sounds like we're talking about something bigger than a single campaign, here."

"We are."

Her cell phone rang, breaking the sudden silence.

"Want me to get that?" Gloria asked softly.

"No. I will." Jessie jogged across the room and dived for her phone to see who was calling. "It's the doctor's office," she told Gloria.

"Well? Answer it!"

"Right." Jessie swiped the screen, hoping she had beaten her voicemail system. "Hi, this is Jessie."

"Jessie, hi. I'm so glad I caught you. This is Dr. Davies."

"Hi, Doc. Listen, I know I need to come back in and talk to you about a treatment plan. I've just been really busy..."

"Jessie?"

"What?"

"I have something to tell you. Do me a favor and find yourself a seat first, okay?"

Jessie's heart dropped. What could be so bad that she needed to sit down? She already knew she had cancer. How much worse could it get?

She dropped down on to the edge of her desk chair. "Okay, I'm sitting."

"Thank you. Listen, there's no easy way to say this, but the biopsy results we were looking at the other day...they weren't yours."

Jessie forgot to breathe. "What do you mean, they weren't mine?"

Gloria trotted over and sat on the edge of her desk. "What's going on?" she mouthed.

Jessie shrugged and put the phone on speaker.

"There was a mix-up in the lab," Dr. Davies was saying. "I don't know how it happened, and I've already fired all the technicians who were on duty that day, but that doesn't excuse it."

"Dr. Davies?"

"Yes?"

"What were the results of *my* biopsy?"

"Your biopsy was negative."

Gloria and Jessie stared at each other, mouths open.

"What does that mean?"

"It means you don't have cancer. The lump is benign. We still need to get it out, but you're healthy."

"I don't have cancer?"

"You don't have cancer."

Jessie dropped the phone and grabbed her sister. "Did you hear that? I don't have cancer!"

Gloria grinned, tears pouring down her face. "No, you don't. You don't have cancer!"

Suddenly they were both on their feet, jumping up and down with excitement like they had when they were five.

"I'm not dying! I'm not dying! Oh, God, Gloria, it's like somebody just gave me my life back!"

Gloria giggled and pretended to hold a microphone up to Jessie's mouth. "Jessie Owens, you've just found out that this is the first day of the rest of your life. What are you going to do with it?"

Jessie didn't even have to think about it. She knew what she wanted to do.

"I'm going to sell Roar. Then I'm going to get Nick back."

Gloria stopped laughing and stared.

"You're going to do what?"

Jessie laughed. "I'm going to sell Roar and get my man back!"

"What? You're moving too fast for me to keep up."

"I've just been given a second chance, Gloria. I don't want to spend it stuck in the dark behind a desk. And I don't want to spend my life alone because I'm afraid of getting hurt. I want to *live*!"

"And to do that you have to sell Roar? Are you sure?"

"I've never been surer of anything in my life."

"And you want Nick back?"

"Yes. Yes, I do."

"All right, then," Gloria said. "Let's sell this sucker and reel in a man."

"These are your conditions?"

Jessie looked at her gray-haired adversary across her lime-green conference table and nodded. "If you want Roar, you'll have to agree to every single term and condition in this agreement."

Brad Thornton looked at her with the same sapphire-blue eyes he had gifted to his son and started ticking things off on his fingers.

"So I have to name Nick CEO of Thornton & Co.?"

"Yes."

"And I have to name Gloria Creative Director?"

"With the same salary you offered me."

He nodded. "And I have to agree to adjust the composition of Thornton's senior management team to include at least five women at all times?"

"That is non-negotiable."

"Understood. But are you really serious about this one? You want me to take half of the fifty million I was prepared to give you for Roar and establish a Thornton Scholarship Fund for women interested in a career in advertising?"

"What can I say? I like irony," she said, unable to hide the smile twitching at the corners of her mouth.

He snorted. "And this last one? This too?"

Jessie nodded.

"I have to agree to stop interfering in your relationship with my son and bless your marriage if and when you decide to take that step?"

"I insist on it."

He leaned back in his chair and looked at her silently for long enough that Jessie began to get worried.

"All right, Jessie. You have a deal. Where do I sign?"

Her lawyer swung into action, producing a pen and showing him where to initial and sign.

Jessie looked at her watch. "Do you need me here for this next part?"

Her lawyer shook his head and smiled. "No. You can sign the documents later. I know you have someplace else you need to be."

"Thank you," she said, and gathered her things.

She was just about to escape through the door when Brad spoke.

"Jessie?"

"Yes?"

"My son is usually a pain in my ass, but I love him. And he deserves a girl like you. Don't let him get away—do you hear me?"

"Loud and clear," she said, saluting as she went out the door.

Nick swore at his friend as he sped away from the marina. "Slow down, Mark! You're going to kill us!"

"No, I'm not. Trust me. Detroit drivers are way scarier than New York drivers. This is a piece of cake."

"If you say so. Where are we going, anyway?"

"To my hotel, and then to the barber shop."

"Why?"

Mark cocked an eyebrow at him. "Because you smell like beer and you look like a troll."

"So?"

"So if I'm going to be seen in public with you you need to get cleaned up."

Nick crossed his arms. He knew he was acting like a petulant child, but he didn't care. "Who said I even wanted to go out?"

"Certainly not you. But I'm only here for one night, and I haven't seen you in more than three months. So we're going out."

Nick grumbled but stayed quiet. He knew he smelled. And he knew that holing up on the yacht, wondering how he could have handled the Jessie situation better, wasn't getting him anywhere. But there wasn't anywhere else he wanted to be. Except with Jessie, of course, but she'd made it clear that she didn't want him anywhere near her.

"So what happened, anyway?" Mark asked.

"What do you mean?"'

"Hold on." Mark darted across four lanes of traffic into a parking spot, narrowly missing a woman pushing a stroller.

"Jeez, Mark. I hope you don't drive like that when Becky's in the car."

Mark pulled up the parking brake and gave him a cocky smile. "Don't worry—she's worse. But back to you. Last time we talked you told me a hot redhead took you to Florida with her for the weekend and you thought you'd found the woman you were going to marry. Fast forward three weeks and I'm scraping you off the floor of your boat. I'm assuming there was an important step in the middle that I wasn't privy to?"

"All right—I'll tell you. But don't call me an idiot when I'm done."

"I won't."

Nick launched into the story as they exited the car. By the time he'd finished they were standing outside Mark's penthouse suite.

"Oh, Nick…"

He hung his head. "I know."

"I can't believe she had to handle that on the same day she'd found out she had cancer."

Nick's head snapped up. "What did you say?"

"That same day you were cooking up your idiotic plan."

"You promised not to call me an idiot."

"I didn't. You're not. That proposal was idiotic."

Nick felt his temper spike. "Whatever. What's this about cancer?"

"While you were planning on stopping at the jewelry store she was at her doctor's office, finding out that she had breast cancer."

"Jessie has cancer? How bad is it?"

No wonder she had reacted that way. She'd needed love and support. He'd offered her what sounded like a business arrangement. What an ass he'd been.

"Oh, don't worry. She doesn't," Mark said, scanning the card that would let them into his suite. "But she thought she did when you were having that dinner. So your proposal was salt in the wound, so to speak."

Nick stepped through the door, then stopped.

"So she doesn't have cancer?"

"No."

"But she thought she did?"

"Yeah.'

"Wait. So you already knew the whole story?" Nick felt his temper start to spike.

"Of course. Becky's her best friend."

"Then why did you make me tell you again?"

"I thought it might sound less idiotic coming from you. I was wrong."

Nick felt something in his brain snap. He hauled off and punched Mark, not even realizing he was doing it until his fist was buried in his stomach.

Mark doubled over, gasping in pain. "Go get in the shower before I clock you," he said.

Nick thought about apologizing, but realized he wasn't ready. Instead he shuffled into the shower.

Jessie was fussing with a string of fairy lights, trying to get them to drape a little more gracefully over a palm leaf, when she heard a familiar voice behind her.

"Your baggage has been collected and is being cleaned up."

"Becky!" she shrieked, clambering down from the ladder so she could hug her blond-haired friend. "You have no idea how glad I am to see you!"

186

"Not as glad as I am to see *you*. I forgot how atrocious New York traffic is. I wasn't sure I'd make it here alive!"

Jessie swept her arms out wide. "So? What do you think?"

Becky grinned. "I think it looks like paradise. I can't believe this is the same building that housed the Happy Hour. How did you get it done so fast? It's been less than a week!"

Jessie shrugged. "When you have millions of dollars to play with you can buy miracles."

"No kidding? Are you at all sorry that you sold Roar?"

"No way. I'm just sorry you couldn't have been there to see Brad Thornton's face when I told him he had to start a scholarship fund. It was priceless."

A shadow crossed her face as she thought about the younger Thornton.

"Did Mark say how Nick seemed?"

"Terrible. Especially after Mark called him an idiot for proposing to you that way."

Jessie giggled. "He didn't?"

"He sure did!" Becky's phone buzzed. "And they're about to be on their way. Better get this party started!"

Jessie nodded. "All right. But, Becky?"

"Yeah?"

"Do you think I'm doing the right thing?"

Becky gave her friend a quick hug. "I think you're doing the rightest possible thing. You guys are made for each other."

Jessie smiled. She thought so too. She only hoped Nick agreed.

"I don't know, man. I don't really feel like going to a club. I think I should go talk to Jessie," Nick said as they got out of the car again, this time inside a parking garage.

Mark scowled at him. "I thought I already made it clear that I don't care what you want? You are not in the proper frame of mind to make decisions. And Jessie doesn't want to talk to you. We're going to the club."

Nick huffed. "Fine. But you're buying all the beer."

"Deal."

Mark hustled him down the stairs and out into the unusually warm April night.

"So where are we going?"

"Right here," Mark said, pointing at a bright pink building.

The only sign was an old white towel with "Paradise" written on it in purple glitter paint.

Something about it looked familiar, but Nick couldn't put his finger on it. "This doesn't look like your usual sort of place."

Mark shrugged. "A friend told me I should try it the next time I was in town."

"All right," Nick said, deciding it was best not to argue.

Mark gave their names to the bouncer at the door and they were waved in. A hostess dressed in a lime-green bikini top and a flamingo-printed sarong greeted them as they walked inside.

"Nick Thornton?" she said, looking directly at him.

He nodded, surprised that she seemed to care.

"Come right this way."

He followed her into the club. Sand covered the floor, and fairy lights twinkled from the branches of the fake palms that stood in front of the blue-painted walls.

"This is amazing," he said to the hostess, suffering from a strange sort of déjà-vu. "It looks crazily like this restaurant in South Florida I was at a couple weeks ago."

"Does it? What a coincidence," she said. "This is your table right here."

He looked where she pointed. It was by itself at the edge of what was clearly a stage. His mind flashed back to the last time he'd sat by a stage and a flash of pain nearly slayed him. Man, he missed that redhead.

"This doesn't have anything to do with Jessie, does it?"

She smiled. "I wouldn't know."

"Do you know where my friend went?"

"He'll be along in a moment."

Nick shrugged and sat. It had to be a coincidence. Mark had said himself that Jessie didn't want to talk to him.

Seconds later the lights went down. The first chords of a classic heartbreak song reverberated in the club and the voice that haunted his dreams filled the air.

Jessie.

The spotlight was switched on and there she was in her lime-green bikini, dancing around the stage as she sang about margaritas and salt shakers. When the song ended she artfully fell into his lap, still holding a microphone.

"What do you think, good-looking? Was it all my fault?"

He shook his head, unable to believe this was happening. "No, it was mine," he croaked.

She turned her attention to the audience. "Did you hear that, people? He said it was *his* fault. What should we make him do?"

"Sing! Sing! Sing!"

"That's right. Here at Paradise we *sing* our way out of trouble. And I know just the song I'd like to sing with you. Will you play along?"

She turned away from the audience and he saw how scared she was.

"Please?" she said quietly, with the microphone down at her side. "I express myself better through song."

He nodded. "Of course."

Grinning, she picked up her microphone. "He said yes, friends!"

The crowd went wild.

"Hit it, DJ Derek!"

The speakers started playing a softer, quieter tune, this one about love found and then too quickly lost. Jessie's voice breathed new life into the words, and he knew she was singing just for him. Her eyes drew him in like a magnet, and by the time the verse faded into the first chorus they were standing hand in hand on stage. He added his voice to hers, forgetting about the audience, the microphone, and even the club as they promised each other second chances and lifelong romances.

When the final notes faded away she threw herself into his arms and planted a desperate, hungry kiss on him. He answered in kind, lifting her up and spinning her in a circle as they kissed.

"I've missed you," she whispered.

"Not nearly as much as I missed you," he answered.

"If we're going to make this work you have to promise to take good care of Roar."

"I don't know what you're talking about."

"You will. Just promise."

"Fine. I promise."

"And just so you know—I still won't marry you."

"I promise not to ask you to for at least another month."

"Good. I love you, Nick Thornton."

"Not as much as I love you, Jessie Owens."

"Prove it."

"I intend to spend the rest of my life doing just that."

"Good. You can take me into my office and start right now."

"I thought you'd never ask."

* * * * *

BOOK_SUBS_2014